THE MASKS OF AUNTIE LAVEAU

A GIL AND CLAIRE HUNT MYSTERY

ROBERT J. RANDISI
CHRISTINE MATTHEWS

**WOLFPACK
PUBLISHING**
— EST 2013 —

BOOKS BY ROBERT J. RANDISI AND
CHRISTINE MATTHEWS

Gil and Claire Hunt Mysteries

Murder Is The Deal of the Day

The Masks of Auntie Laveau

Same Time, Same Murder

Published in the United States by Wolfpack Publishing, Las Vegas.

Wolfpack Publishing
6032 Wheat Penny Avenue
Las Vegas, NV 89122

wolfpackpublishing.com

Paperback ISBN: 978-1-64119-441-9
Ebook ISBN: 978-1-64119-440-2

Library of Congress Control Number: 2018960488

THE MASKS OF AUNTIE LAVEAU

To that old black magic

CHAPTER 1

"DON'T YOU DARE bring me back to this wicked place again," Claire said.

"I didn't bring you," Gil answered. "You brought me, remember?"

Actually, the television station Claire Hunt worked for had sent her to New Orleans and she, in turn, had invited Gil. After cashing in her first-class airline ticket, they had used the money to rent a car. Road trips were one of their favorite ways of spending time together. And the station was paying for a hotel room, whether she was in it alone, or with her husband. It had all worked out perfectly.

Gil had agreed immediately to accompany her for two reasons: the French Quarter had great used-book stores, and he would have missed her too much if he'd stayed home.

"Semantics," she scolded, "you're always hitting me with semantics. The point is, don't ever let me come here again."

"Why not?"

"Because," she said, biting into her hot dog, "all I've done since we arrived is eat."

"We only got here yesterday, Claire."

"And already I've had rice and beans, cheesecake—the best cheesecake I ever had—étouffée, beignets, and now a Lucky Dog."

They were in Jackson Square at lunchtime. The place was bustling with palm readers, magicians, tarot-card readers, sketch artists displaying canvases on park benches, and vendors selling soft drinks, hot dogs, ice cream, popcorn and candy.

Surrounding the square on all four sides were restaurants, cafés, gift shops, jewelry stores, and antique shops. Tourists strolled, snapping pictures of everything. And while all of this took place in the shadow of the beautiful Saint Louis Cathedral, Gil and Claire stood in the midst of it—eating.

"I'm getting fat," she said. "I can feel myself swelling up as we speak. The camera is going to make me look like a gigantic blowfish."

"You don't go on camera until tomorrow," Gil said. "Just fast until then." He shrugged. "Simple."

"Are you crazy? We're in the Big Easy, baby. We still have lots to see and many meals to eat."

In truth, she looked as blond and beautiful as ever, but he'd never be able to convince her of that.

"Speaking of places to go," he said, "don't we have to meet that Mask Lady today?"

The Mask Lady, as they had come to refer to the mysterious woman, had called Claire direct in Saint Louis. She told her that she had heard The Home Shopping Mall was coming to do a live program in New Orleans. She was an artist and had a "special item" she was sure the viewers would be interested in.

"You're the only host me trusts," the woman had said, in a heavy Jamaican accent Claire had found utterly charming. "I can tell all I need to know about a person from looking into their eyes. You have honest eyes, girl."

Claire was flattered.

The woman described the miniature Mardi Gras masks to Claire, who was intrigued, and after consulting with her products coordinator, had agreed to meet the woman personally.

"She's supposed to leave a message at the hotel."

Gil looked at his watch. "It's one o'clock. Do you want to walk down Bourbon Street before we head back?"

"You know I do."

She finished her Coke. "God, whoever invented this stuff was a genius."

At that moment a call was coming in to the hotel for Claire Hunt. When the caller was told Mrs. Hunt was not in her room, she decided to leave a message.

"Tell her Auntie Laveau called."

"Laveau?" The hotel operator's voice seemed amused, but Auntie was used to that.

"You just tell her I'll be meetin' her at Ol' Number One at five o'clock."

"I'll be sure to tell her, ma'am."

Auntie hung up the phone, shaking her head. As she started to rise from the table, she heard a noise from the back room of her small A-frame home on the point of Algiers.

"Who's dere?" she called out, approaching the doorway. As she entered the room, a blow to the back of her head kept her from repeating the question. She crashed to the floor and never felt the rain of blows that followed . . . the first one had been enough to kill her.

CHAPTER 2

AIR-CONDITIONING BLEW NICE AND COLD. Tossing her packages in a corner, Claire plopped down on the bed. It was Gil who noticed the message light blinking on the phone and called the front desk.

"With all the research you've done preparing for this trip, do you remember coming across the name Laveau?" he asked, after relaying the message to her.

"You mean Marie Laveau? The Voodoo Queen?"

He stood in front of the opened shutters, admiring the view from their third-floor room. They were at the Saint Ann-Marie Antoinette Hotel on Rue de Conte, which put them half a block from both Bourbon and Royale streets. At night they could hear the music and voices emanating from Bourbon Street until well into the morning. Gil thoroughly enjoyed the beat and pulse of that famous street, but Claire preferred to experience both from a civilized distance.

She rubbed her feet. The temperature had risen to an unseasonable, un-October-like ninety-five degrees and she was convinced she had packed all the wrong clothes for the trip. Gil looked slightly wilted from the high humidity, but he was always warm, no matter the season, no matter what clothing he wore.

"Suppose she could be a distant relative. Are there any relatives left?" she asked him. Not only did her husband own a bookstore but Claire was convinced he had read every book on every shelf.

"Marie had one daughter. Could be some great-great-grandchildren around, I guess. All the stories I've read seem to contradict each other, though. No telling what the truth is."

Claire walked over to see what was holding her husband's attention.

"They should call this the shuttered city," Gil commented.

"It certainly has charm. I guess we should ask the desk clerk where and what Old Number One is."

"It's a cemetery," Gil said. "Saint Louis Cemetery Number One. The voodoo queen is buried there."

Claire rolled her eyes. "Artists can be so temperamental."

"There's a tour. It starts from Pirates Alley, where I found the Faulkner House bookstore. I wanted to take it tomorrow but we might as well see if we can catch it today. Then we won't be alone out there at five o'clock when Auntie shows up."

It was their first visit to New Orleans and the French Quarter, but it didn't surprise her that Gil already had his bearings. He had a phenomenal memory when it came to directions, while she relied on the "always turn right" rule to get back to where she started. It worked best in malls.

"Now?" she moaned. "But we just got back and it's so hot . . ."

"If I remember correctly . . ."

"And you always do . . ." she interrupted.

". . . there's a praline shop where groups gather to start the tour. I saw signs while I was eating."

"You ate something without me?"

"Come on," he said, ignoring the gibe, "change into that sexy cotton thingie you just bought, the one with the V-neck?" He smiled and held out his hands to her, palms up in that graceful way she loved, to help her off the bed. She complained just a little more, couldn't have him thinking she was so easily swayed by his logic—or his charm—even though she usually was.

CHAPTER 3

THE SUN BURNED in the sky and Claire was miserable following a tour guide who carried a large black umbrella. As they crossed Rampart Street and left the Quarter, they ended up on Basin Street. The group of fifteen was cautioned that respect was required. An awkward silence overtook them and after listening to the history of the area, they were led along a worn path snaking through the crowded cemetery until they found themselves standing in front of the large stone tomb of Marie Laveau.

A red candle had been stuck in a mason jar. As it burned in the intense daylight, it blackened the container. Pennies were propped on a ledge above Laveau's name and a few flowers, all dead now, were scattered on the ground in front of the crumbling monument. Someone had even left an unopened bottle of flavored iced tea. Hundreds of red lipstick Xs were scrawled on every available piece of granite.

When Gil asked about them, the guide shook her head sadly. "Somehow the story got started that if you want a wish granted, you mark three crosses on Marie's tomb and it will come true. It's a shame how it all got out of hand. Please do not touch anything. The caretaker has to clean up this mess every night."

"What about the bottle of iced tea?" Claire asked.

The guide shook her head again. "People will leave anything as a tribute."

After a few more minutes, the group was led down a narrow path toward a large Italian monument. The guide began to explain how the cast and crew of the movie *Easy Rider* had broken into the cemetery to shoot a scene there after they'd been denied permission. Gil didn't want Claire to know it but he was just as uncomfortable as she. As he looked for a shady spot, he thought about a cold beer in a frosty mug. The guide began talking again, this time about burial techniques in Louisiana, and Gil's mind wandered. Claire startled him when she whispered, "I've had enough. How about we sit out the rest of this tour and wait for the Mask Lady over there?" She pointed to a bench near the entrance.

"Fine with me," he said, unable to hide the sweat on his brow and under his arms.

The guide shot Gil and Claire a dirty look as she led the rest of her group outside the heavy gates and back across the street. The heat must have gotten to the young woman also, because when Claire looked at her watch she noticed there was fifteen minutes remaining of tour time.

At precisely five o'clock, a woman carrying a brightly colored tote bag approached the couple.

"Mrs. Hunt?"

"Auntie Laveau?" Claire asked hesitantly as she stood to greet the woman.

"I knew dat was you, I was sure dat was you. Why, I told myself as soon I rounded the corner, 'dat's the pretty lady from the television.' I bet people are all the time tellin' you how lovely you look in person."

Claire laughed uncomfortably. "Well, some have."

Gil stood and extended his hand. "Ms. Laveau, I'm Claire's husband, Gil."

"So nice to meet you." The thin woman shook his hand with everything she had. "So very nice."

"Can we take you someplace cooler to talk?" Claire asked hopefully. "We could have a drink and look at the masks you made. I assume you've brought a few with you?"

"Right here." She patted the bag. "I know, let's go down the street to the Napoleon."

Before either one could agree or offer an alternative, the woman marched ahead, leading them like a mother duck.

"Something's wrong," Claire whispered. "All the books I've read describe Marie Laveau as 'a woman of color.' She doesn't look like even a distant relative."

"I read Marie was a mulatto," Gil whispered back.

"Her skin's white as milk," Claire said. "And her accent's . . . wrong."

"Well," Gil said, "we're going to a public place. If something doesn't feel right, we'll leave. Look at her, Claire, she must be at least sixty—and I bet you outweigh her by, uh, twenty pounds. Don't worry, if she starts anything, I think you can take her."

Claire did not laugh.

CHAPTER 4

CLAIRE HAD HOPED the café would be air-conditioned but instead found herself in a quaint old building situated on a busy corner. The front door as well as all the shutters had been propped open. They sat in a dark corner, a ceiling fan buzzed, making the temperature in the room bearable. At least they were out of the direct sunlight. The plastered walls were the color of tea, a generous assortment of liqueur bottles decorated shelves behind and above the bar.

After they ordered, the woman opened her bag and brought out a purple velvet pouch. She handled it as though the contents were priceless.

"I work hard, Mrs. Hunt." Since Claire was the one she had the appointment with, the woman was obviously going to address her. "Very hard. I paint every detail by hand."

Claire picked up the ceramic mask that had been placed with such care in front of her on the table. She handled it respectfully while bringing it in close for a thorough examination.

It was as small as her thumbprint, painted with a translucent coating. The white face had exaggerated black eyelashes, a pink blotch dabbed on each cheek. The lips were painted red and the forehead was detailed with one large rose surrounded by three tiny violets. On the very top was a small gold loop through which a pink ribbon had been strung. When Claire turned the Mardi Gras face over, she saw it was unfinished except for the name "Kelly Denoux," painted in black.

"How many of these do you have finished?" Claire asked.

"Two hundred," the woman said proudly.

"I'll have to take this with me, to show our product coordinator."

The woman looked confused. "But . . . I thought we had a deal. You agreed to see me. Why would you do that if we didn't have a deal?"

Gil was startled by the woman's sudden agitation and could see his wife needed help. "The program doesn't air until later in the week, Ms. Laveau. Claire has to take your product to her buyer. It's just routine."

"In fact, if we want to get your delightful masks featured, I'll have to hurry and try to catch him right now."

The waiter arrived, unloaded his tray and walked away. "Gil, could you get the check?" Claire asked.

"But we haven't had our drinks yet."

Claire tried signaling him without offending the woman beside her. "Miss Laveau has worked so hard, and if we leave now we might be able to get Steve to make a decision tonight." She was using her tone and eyes to hurry him along. Turning to the artist, Claire smiled. "I'll call you first thing in the morning so you won't have to wait any longer. I hate waiting, waiting, always waiting for other people to make decisions about my life. Don't you hate that?"

"You're very thoughtful, Mrs. Hunt, but I have a new number. Let me give it to you."

Gil could see that at the rate the old woman moved it would take her an eternity to find a pen, let alone a scrap of paper. "Here"—he opened his wallet and pulled out a business card—"write on the back of this. Claire, do you have a pen?"

Auntie Laveau grabbed the card.

Frustrated, and tugging at his elbow, Claire said, "I know. You have our number at the hotel; why don't you just give us a call tomorrow afternoon?"

The woman smiled a broad smile that showed one tooth missing in the front, on the bottom. "Dat I will do." Claire abruptly stood up. Putting her hand on the woman's bony shoulder, she pressed her down into her seat. "Don't get up. Relax, enjoy your beer. No need you rushing off just because we have to."

"Thank you. Thank you very much." Auntie Laveau rearranged her oversized black dress. Then, lifting her large glass, she watched the couple as they walked to the bar to pay the bill, then out the front door.

Gil had to run to keep up with his wife. "Sorry I was so thick. Want to tell me what's going on?"

"Just walk. Hurry. Act as though we're in a rush to get somewhere. Not like there's something wrong."

"Something's wrong?"

"I'm not sure. I won't feel safe until we get to the hotel."

Closing the door behind him, Gil gulped for air. "Was it necessary to run up three flights? What's wrong with the elevator?" He tried taking his wife's intuition in stride, but sometimes she just baffled him. She always told him he should be thankful, that it was her gut feelings that would always keep them safe. He had to take her at her word.

"What should we do?" Claire asked, pacing.

"About what? Gil grabbed his wife and held her tightly. She was beginning to scare him. "Honey, about what? Tell me."

"That woman's a fake, Gil. I'm positive."

"I thought so, too, but how can you be so sure? You've never met her before."

They sat down together on the edge of the bed.

"First off, she didn't seem to remember I told her, or whoever it was I spoke to on the phone, that we need one thousand pieces of a product."

"She could have forgotten. Maybe she's just absent-minded."

"What about her accent?" Claire asked. "On the phone it was charming, pretty. Did you notice how it came and went? And it was far from charming."

"I did notice that, yes."

"And look at this." Claire took the mask out of her pocket. "Who's Kelly Denoux? The woman I spoke to on the phone said she made the masks—all of them—herself."

"Maybe Denoux is the woman's real name," Gil said. "Maybe she just calls herself Auntie Laveau." He examined the signature on the rough plaster. "It could have been made especially for someone and she just brought it along as a sample."

"Okay, then look at this." Claire got up and opened the top drawer of the dresser. Taking out a paper bag, she removed a small white box. "I bought this yesterday, at the first shop we stopped at." She held out the box to her husband.

Gil lifted the lid, removed a layer of cotton to find a

small mask, almost identical to the one in his palm. After examining and comparing the two, he looked up at Claire. "So, she sells them to stores around town."

"When I bought that one"—she pointed to the box—"it was the first one I had ever seen. But then we shopped all day and I saw them everywhere. On street corners, in hotel gift shops; I even saw a display in one of your bookstores. And look at that rose on the head. It's a decal, not hand-painted. This woman must think we're blind or stupid not to see all the masks everywhere and naive to think hers are special."

"So she's just a little . . . odd. And not particularly talented." Gil couldn't help but notice the inferior quality of the mask the woman had given them. "But none of this seems reason enough for you to be so upset, making us run back here."

Before she could offer up more reasons to defend her actions than just a feeling deep in the pit of her stomach that something was very, very wrong, that something bad was going to happen, the phone rang, startling them both.

"Don't answer it." Claire whispered.

"Calm down," he said, but made no move toward the phone.

They sat on the bed, staring. Gil wondered how to handle the situation and was ready to try reasoning with his wife. He started to open his mouth when someone knocked loudly on their door before the echo of the last ring had faded away, startling them even more.

"What do you want me to do now?" Gil asked.

"Mrs. Hunt?" a man's voice said discreetly into the door. "It's Mr. Pickett, the manager."

"You answer it . . . please," Claire pleaded.

Gil checked himself in the large mirror hanging above the dresser. "Just a moment," he yelled.

The man standing in the hallway looked embarrassed. "Sorry to disturb you, Mr. Hunt. Something happened this afternoon while you were out. I'd like to come in and speak with you and Mrs. Hunt . . . privately."

"Of course." Gil stood back, allowing the man to enter. After Mr. Pickett had walked into the room, Gil locked the door.

Claire had retreated into the bathroom. When she came out she appeared calmer.

After introductions and apologies were made, Mr. Pickett explained. "The police were here, looking for you. They wanted me to let them into your room, but of course I refused." Claire couldn't help but stare at the nervous man's mustache, noticing how it fluttered each time he exhaled an exasperated breath. "They gave me this card and asked that I have you call them."

"Thank you," Claire said, taking it.

"They never mentioned what they wanted from us?" Gil asked.

Mr. Pickett nodded. "They said it was just routine. Not that I would know what their routine was, but no mention was made of an emergency of any sort. Please be assured that I and my staff are at your disposal." Then the man retreated to the door. While turning the dead bolt several times he apologized again, opened the door and quickly exited.

The couple stared at each other for a moment, but before either had a chance to speak, the phone started ringing again.

This time Claire marched across the room and grabbed

the receiver. Gil knew that, along with everything else that was going on, she was thinking about her son, Paul.

"Yes?" she asked. "Who is it?"

"Finally! Where the hell have you been? Don't you check messages? I thought you just got a cell phone. How is anyone supposed to get ahold of you if you don't turn the thing on?"

Claire held her hand over the mouthpiece. "It's Steve," she told Gil, and then spoke into the phone. "Tell me what's so urgent and then I'll tell you my news."

"Your news can't be as big as mine."

"So tell me already," Claire insisted.

"That Auntie Laveau person you and Gil met this afternoon? She's dead!"

CHAPTER 5

DETECTIVE LASALLE, OF the New Orleans Police Department, had agreed to meet them in the small bar in the courtyard of the hotel later that night. It was less crowded after dinner and offered more comfort than their small room. The ambience was also calming and Claire found herself relaxing a little as she watched a small boy skim across the top of the blue water in the pool.

LaSalle arrived a few minutes early. He was younger than he'd sounded on the phone when they'd made the appointment. And rounder. Gil figured the man must be mainly responsible for paperwork and interviewing.

When the couple were asked about the reason for their visit, Gil did the talking. They had learned, over the few years they'd been together, each other's weaknesses and strengths. When an unusual circumstance arouse, the one better suited for the task at hand took the lead. At the moment, that was Gil.

After their itinerary had been laid out in full for the policeman, it was Claire who lost her patience first and blurted out, "So, Detective, why are you here?"

So much for the one better suited to the task doing the talking, Gil thought.

"There's been a murder, Mrs. Hunt," LaSalle replied. "A woman claiming to be Auntie Laveau was killed early this morning."

"Claiming?" she asked.

"There are quite a few people here in New Orleans who swear they're descendants of the Voodoo Queen." The detective looked up from his notebook and grinned. "It's good for the tourists—helps ease more money out of their pockets."

"Do you believe any of them?" Gil asked.

"I don't think about it long enough to have much of an opinion, Mr. Hunt." Referring back to his notes, the detective read, "The woman we found this morning was a two-hundred-pound Jamaican, sixty years old. She had resided at the same address in Algiers since 1946. She was known by all her neighbors as Marie Laveau. Apparently her real name was Cleo Laveau." He looked at them. "I suppose having that last name made it easy for her to claim to be related." Back to his notes. "We found yellow Post-It notes stuck to everything. She either had a terrible memory or a very strange way of decorating." He laughed slightly at his own joke, but continued when neither Gil nor Claire joined in. "Seventeen of those notes referred to both of you, Mrs. Hunt, or the station you work for—The Home Mall?—along with today's date. If it wasn't for the fact that one of my men watches the program you host— says his wife is a big fan, by the way—we wouldn't have gotten to you at all today."

"I knew it!" Claire exclaimed. "I knew the woman we met today wasn't the same person I talked to last week." She looked at LaSalle. "She was very tiny, pale complexion, over sixty, and had a phony Jamaican accent."

"So you were scheduled to meet with the victim today?"

"Yes," Claire said, "at least, I think it was her. It certainly wasn't the woman we ended up meeting."

"Did this woman present herself to you as Marie Laveau?" LaSalle asked.

"Well, no, we just assumed that's who she was—but she never contradicted us," Gil said. "Come to think of it, she never did say what her name was. But she talked as if she was the one who had spoken to Claire on the phone."

"May I see what it was she brought to show you?"

Claire removed the mask from her purse and handed it to him.

"Kelly Denoux," the detective read aloud.

"Do you know who she is?" Claire asked.

"Haven't a clue," the man said, "but I'll take this with me and check it out. You were meeting with her about featuring this item on your show?"

"Yes."

"You can get these anywhere in the Quarter—and of better quality."

"We know that now," Claire said sheepishly.

He dropped it into his handkerchief and tucked it away. "I still have that woman's phone number," Claire said. "Should we call her and set up another meeting? Try to trap . . . ?"

"No, ma'am, that won't be necessary. Just give me the number and you and your husband will be out of it."

She handed him the card with Auntie Laveau's number written on it.

"Can either of you think of anything else I should know?"

Gil and Claire exchanged a glance and then Gil said, "No, we've told you everything."

"Okay, then I'd appreciate it if you didn't leave town just yet. I might have some more questions for you."

"Is that really necessary?" Gil asked. "We both have to get back to work, and it's not as if we were suspects . . . or are we?"

LaSalle thought it over for a few seconds and then said, "Well, if you'll just give me your home phone number and assure me that you'll come back if we need you to . . ."

"That wouldn't be a problem," Gil said. "We'd be glad to help, if we can."

While Claire wrote their number down on the card LaSalle handed her, she was having flashbacks from the last time she and Gil had tried "helping" the police. Actually, they'd had to clear Claire's name when someone was killing women in their apartments and leaving behind VCR tapes of Claire on television. She had ended up being questioned, suspected, insulted and kidnapped.

"I'll say good-bye, then," LaSalle said. "I have some other people to see."

"Of course," Gil said, shaking his hand.

Once the man was out of sight, Claire said, "I think I'm ready to go home now."

"No argument here," Gil said.

CHAPTER 6

AS SHE DROVE into the parking garage beneath their condo, Claire turned to poke Gil, who dozed in the passenger seat. "Wake up, Sleeping Beauty, we're here."

"Huh? Where?" He removed his sunglasses and rubbed his eyes. She watched him try to find the lever that would pop his seat into the upright position. His frustration with ordinary tasks always amused her.

"Home. At last!" She leaned over to kiss him. "It feels like we've been away for years instead of just a week."

"I thought you loved to travel." He got out and slammed his door. She was already starting to pull luggage from the trunk.

Claire handed him a garment bag. "Sure, when it doesn't include days of live remotes in the blazing sun, oh, and don't forget . . . the police interviewing us about a murder. Death always puts a damper on things for me."

Loaded down, they walked slowly to the elevator.

"Aww, come on, now," Gil teased, "you're always telling me how you're such a people person. Just think of Detective LaSalle as your new best friend. All that stuff about him knowing somebody whose wife liked your show . . . I'll bet he's the fan."

"You can be so strange sometimes." Claire pushed the button for their floor and the elevator doors closed.

"That's what you love about me the most, right, baby?" His comments hadn't made her laugh, but she grinned. Close enough.

After dropping the luggage in their bedroom, Claire went to the dining room and pulled back the curtains. Their balcony overlooked Brentwood Avenue and the Park. Claire bent to unlock the bolt near the floor and then slid open the heavy glass door.

October in Saint Louis could be tricky. She had learned long ago not to get fooled by the cool September evenings. The first few years she'd lived in the city, she'd packed her summer clothes away weeks before Halloween, only to find herself rummaging around in the back of her closet for something to wear. One day the temperature would climb into the high eighties and the very next she'd have to pull out a heavy sweater. But no matter how long the humidity and heat hung on, the city offered a pleasant relief from the Louisiana mugginess.

Gil walked into the room and began sorting through mail that had been piled on the dining room table.

"Bill. Catalog. Ad. Catalog. We must be on everyone's mailing list. Look at all these catalogs. There's even one here for Celtic clothing."

"Yeah, I'll have to remember to thank Paul for bringing it all in while we were gone."

"That son of yours is a good kid," Gil said, leafing

through a catalog advertising products made in Vermont. "We have to get over and see his new place."

Claire walked out onto the balcony and inhaled the cool evening air. The sun was setting, highlighting clouds with streaks of gold and pink. She watched the cars below crawl along busy streets. "It's so good to have him close by. Kansas City was too far away."

Gil pushed the mail aside and went to join his wife. "Wow, it feels great out here," he said, coming up behind her. "I keep forgetting how green everything still is."

Claire turned to curl her arms around his waist. "You have a lot of catching up to do down at the bookstore."

"Now that all our inventory's on a computer, I get the feeling things can run themselves down there without the old man."

Claire stepped back and looked up at his bearded face. "Old? A few gray hairs here and there don't make you old."

"What about the middle-age spread?" he asked, patting his stomach.

"Watch it there, buddy. If you're middle-aged, what am I?"

He buried his nose in her fragrant golden hair. "You're the older, exciting woman in my life."

"Older? Three years, big deal. Besides, women don't get older, they get more valuable."

"That's a good one," he agreed.

"You're just feeling overwhelmed about hitting the big four-oh."

He was thinking of a snappy comeback when a fire truck raced through the streets below. Both turned to watch. An ambulance rounded a corner and two police cars joined the procession. The screeching sirens were deafening.

Claire released Gil and headed back inside. "Whenever

I hear sirens I always think that they signal the worst day in someone's life. And I feel guilty because I'm happy, or that at this time in my life, I don't have any real problems."

Gil closed the door. "I know what you mean. I can't stop thinking about that poor woman in New Orleans. How someone not only killed her, but stole her name."

"Which she stole from the real Marie Laveau," Claire pointed out.

"I wonder," Gil said, "how many women have done that over the years."

I wonder if we'll ever find out what happened," Claire said. "Who killed her, and why? Who that other woman was?"

"Well, if you're really interested, that detective gave me his card," Gil said, producing it from his pocket. "I could give him a call and see what he has to—"

He seemed entirely too eager to make the call, so she cut him off. "Don't you dare."

CHAPTER 7

"O MY DEAR MOTHER, your child comes to you with tears in the eyes and a downcast look in the face, for I have lost all that I possessed in this world. My hopes are vanishing and with no one to turn to but you, I therefore implore your help. Restore to me the smile of happiness that once was mine. I would give part of my life for some of the luck that I used to possess. O Mother, will you hear my prayer and help me?"

After reciting the supplication, she took the chamois bag and tucked a piece of lodestone inside. Laying it down on a splintered table beside the altar, she went into the kitchen for the other things she needed.

Returning to the small room in the front of the house, she laid out a piece of John the Conqueror root, a pair of Adam and Eve root and a piece of devil's-shoestring root. After stuffing all ingredients into the bag, she tied it securely, making sure nothing would fall out. Then, holding the bag in her left hand, she sprinkled five drops of holy oil onto it with her right while reciting the Twenty-third

Psalm. When this was done, she reverently placed the small bag into the pocket of her apron.

"I have followed your teachings, Marie Laveau, and now wait for the good luck to return. I pray for your help in keeping away those with too many questions, make them fearful to cross my threshold."

A few of the candles had gone out and she struck a large match. Circling the room, she carefully relit the wicks.

When she was satisfied that everything was right, she opened the large front door and walked out into the New Orleans sun.

CHAPTER 8

THE AMERICAN KENNEL CLUB MUSEUM OF THE DOG was located in Queeny Park, on the western side of Saint Louis. It housed some of the finest paintings, sculptures, rare books and antiques, all gathered to honor man's best friend. Because it was considered to be a premier gallery, Claire was anxious to attend the mystery night organized by her friend Stella Bartlett.

"So what in the world do I wear to a dog museum?" Gil asked, standing in the middle of their bedroom dressed only in his silk Looney Tunes boxer shorts and a smile.

Claire came out of the bathroom buttoning the jacket of her pin-striped suit. "I don't believe you! Here I am all ready—my hair done, makeup on, all dressed, and you haven't even started."

Gil plopped onto the bed. "Just help me out. You know I can be ready in five minutes. Just tell me what to wear." Walking to the closet, she worked her fingers over several hangers until she found what she was looking for. "Here," she said, handing him a black-and-gray tweed jacket. "Gray pants on the bottom and a black, white, or gray shirt on top."

Gil went to his dresser and selected a pair of black socks with the outline of a man and woman dancing knit into the pattern in purple. Holding them up to his wife, he grinned. "How's this for accessorizing?"

"You and those crazy socks." She tossed the clothes onto the bed. "Now get your cute self dressed and meet me in the living room in ten minutes."

A cool mist sprayed down, sparkling in their headlights and causing amber leaves to stick to the winding road leading to the museum. The park surrounding the old mansion that housed the gallery was lit with small floodlights. They were surprised to find very few parking spaces available. As they hurried down the walkway, Claire held her shawl tightly around her shoulders.

"It's getting colder by the minute. I love this kind of weather."

They were greeted by a butler when they entered the lobby. "May I take your wrap?"

"No, I think I'll keep it with me, thank you." Claire wondered if the man came along with the caterer or was an actor.

A petite woman dressed in an elegant black dress approached them. Extending her hand, she said, "Welcome. I'm Barbara Jedda, executive director of the museum."

"I'm Gil Hunt and this is my wife, Claire." They shook her hand.

"You're Stella's friends! She's always talking about you. What a lifesaver she's been, organizing this night for us. The museum operates on donations, and thanks to Stella we're sold out."

"Is she around?" Claire asked. "We've been out of town and I've been dying to tell her all about our trip."

"She's in the main gallery. I'm on my way there now. Come on."

As they walked along the long hallway, Barbara would stop and explain the history of the paintings. Claire was fascinated by the woman and couldn't help noticing how her professional demeanor and dress were contradicted by the black-fringed cowboy boots peeking out from beneath her long dress.

The highly polished floor and strategically placed track lighting drew Claire's attention to a large statue at the end of the hallway standing in front of high bay windows. "This is wonderful!"

Barbara smiled. "That's Queen, our unofficial mascot. I bet you've never seen a carousel dog before. They were manufactured in the late nineteenth century. Very rare— we're lucky to have her."

"It's a mastiff, isn't it?" Gil asked.

"It sure is. We have a collection in the other room donated by a woman who only collected mastiff motifs. There are brooches, pictures, even a beaded evening bag." The curator curled a wisp of auburn hair behind her ear as she spoke. "You'll both have to come back when you have more time and I'll give you a personal guided tour."

They entered the crowded gallery. "We're just the kind of people who'll hold you to that offer," Gil said.

"Claire! Gilberto!" Stella Bartlett came running across the room to enfold Claire into a bear hug. Gil stood back, allowing the women more room to enjoy their reunion. "Get over here, you." Stella released Claire and grabbed Gil. "God, I've missed you! You'll have to tell me all about your trip after we get through this evening." Stella kissed the air around the couple and ran off to catch the waiter holding a tray of champagne glasses.

"Excuse me, I have to get things started. It was so nice meeting you and I hope you do come back when we can have more time." Barbara headed up toward the microphone situated on a small stage. Something told Claire they would become good friends.

The evening turned out to be more fun than they could have imagined. Upstairs galleries had been splashed with bloodied fingerprints and clues which would, it was hoped, lead to a solution to the mystery that had been staged in the main gallery. Each attendee scurried around the museum, trying to figure out who had killed the rich, famous and fictitious Mrs. Vanderluck. At the end of the hour, everyone gathered downstairs in a small meeting room for hors d'oeuvres, cocktails and the solution.

"Think you figured it out?" Claire asked Gil after he came back from depositing his written solution in a box supplied for that purpose.

He folded his arms. "I got it."

A local mystery writer sauntered out in a trench coat and fedora. In grand style he reviewed the case and finally announced the identity of the culprit. An actor playing the part of the guilty gardener tried to escape, but the "detective" was faster and soon had him handcuffed.

"If you'll all please enjoy dessert in the lobby, we'll award prizes to the winners in a few moments."

"Well?" Claire asked Gil as they filed out of the room with the rest of the guests.

"Never mind," he said, obviously miffed that he—the Great Amateur Detective—had not cracked the case.

Claire smiled and held his arm tightly. "That's all right. We're friends of Stella's. If you had won it would have looked fixed."

"Leave it to you to give me an out. So I can assume that you were stumped, too?"

"Well . . . not exactly."

"You mean you knew it was the gardener?"

"It seemed so obvious."

"But what about all that stuff you just said. How we're Stella's friends and it would look fixed . . ."

"Relax. I didn't put my solution in the box. Are you satisfied?"

Gil continued grumbling to himself as they made their way to the lobby.

Little cakes and cookies were served on doily-covered trays. While everyone chatted and waited, Gil struck up a conversation with a tall Jamaican man who introduced himself as Ms. Jedda's husband, Huntley.

"Ah, New Orleans. Such a wonderful city, so full of charm, history."

"So you travel a lot?" Gil asked.

"Oh, most certainly. My job takes me all over the world."

"And you enjoy living in Saint Louis?"

"It's a lovely town. Barbara and I live over in the Central West End."

Claire joined in the conversation. "We live in Clayton. In that high-rise building off Brentwood."

Barbara stepped up to the microphone, causing the threesome to shift their attention. "We have two winners tonight. If Carrie Cafazza and Kathy Morris will come up here, we'll get a few pictures and hand out your prizes."

The two women worked their way excitedly through

the crowd.

"Would you please introduce yourselves to our guests?" The tallest of the two grabbed the microphone, enjoying the spotlight. "I'm Kathy Morris; I work at Gundaker Realtors. I heard about this mystery night only this afternoon, on TV, and thought it would be fun. I'm also the grandmother of three."

It was obvious to everyone how much the woman enjoyed hearing the response of the crowd when they heard the last piece of information, since she looked too young to be anyone's grandmother.

"Thank you, Kathy." Barbara addressed the other woman. "And you must be Carrie."

"Yes, I'm an alderwoman in Ward One, and a flight attendant for TWA. Kathy and I are friends; we decided to come here on the spur of the moment. I've never won anything; this is so exciting!"

"Well, for showing us all what wonderful sleuths you both are, we'd like to present you with gift certificates and T-shirts from our museum store."

Both women accepted the prizes with great appreciation. The audience cheered the women and each took a playful bow.

"I'd like to thank everyone again for attending our first mystery night here at the Museum of the Dog. I'm sure it won't be our last."

A push started toward the doors as people picked up their coats and headed for the parking lot.

"Stella should be very proud of herself," Gil said.

"Yes, she should. Everything went so smoothly."

"It looks like it's really coming down out there. You wait here—I'll pull the car up."

Claire smiled. "I love it when you let me be helpless."

CHAPTER 9

GIL SAT IN front of the television trying to wake up. Eating a bowl of cereal, he stared at the image of his wife while she hosted her morning show on The Home Mall, telecast from a small cable station based in Saint Louis. The scope of the station encompassed quite a large portion of the Midwest, making his wife something of a celebrity.

"It's the start of a new week and I'm all recharged after my trip to the Big Easy. In fact, we've had so many wonderful calls from our viewers that next month Michele and Dan will be heading out to do a program from New Mexico.

"Now for our next item, we have a versatile all-weather coat. Perfect for this time of year. It comes in five colors and is only thirty-nine, ninety-five. Later on we'll be featuring a matching scarf and hat, which our lovely Abby is modeling for us. So be sure to stay tuned . . ."

"Sorry, hon." Gil took one last look at his wife, dressed in her new plum sweater and thought how great she looked. "No can do. Gotta get to the store."

Despite what Gil had said to Claire about his store running itself, he really didn't want it to. Whenever they returned from a trip he was really quite anxious to get back to The Old Delmar Bookstore. Not a very imaginative name, perhaps, since the store was actually on a street named Delmar, in a trendy section of town known as University City, but Gil liked it.

As he entered, he inhaled deeply and smiled. It had been very important to him, when he first contemplated opening a bookstore—after the dissolution of his first marriage and reorganization of his financial situation—that it have the aged, comforting smell of the old bookstores he had haunted as a child. As far as its being a profitable concern, the jury was still out on that one. He did an okay mailorder business, which not only accounted for the majority of his income, but had recently started showing a marked increase in profits since the store had hit the Web. He had some regulars, too, who came in every month, but his walk-in business was still from hunger.

"Welcome back, boss!" his part-time worker shouted. Allyn Marcus was a longtime customer who came in from time to time to cover the store when Gil had to travel. The longer he used the young man, the more duties he'd started to trust him with. In fact, within the last few weeks, he'd started allowing the kid to buy used books while he was away.

"Thanks, Al."

"What's up?" the young man asked from his seated position behind the desk. When Gil had opened the store he'd decided against having a counter, opting for a large oak desk that he'd sit behind so he could talk casually with his customers.

"Not much. How's it been going here? Any problems?"

Al straightened his wire frames. "Nothing I couldn't handle."

Gil smiled and wondered if he had ever appeared as eager and young as Al did now. He hoped so. "Did you plan on working all day?"

"Sure did. No classes until Wednesday. I'm all yours till then."

"We gotta get you a woman, my friend. You have way too much spare time."

"Girls just complicate things; I like my life exactly the way it is."

Gil knew that this was the way men talked when they didn't have a woman in their life. It justified their being alone, but that soon changes when a female enters the picture. He knew that because he had not been looking for a woman at all when Claire came into his life and he wouldn't give up that moment in time for anything.

Gil hung his jacket up on the rack by his dinosaur of a desk. "Do you know offhand if we have any books on voodoo? I want to do some research."

Al shivered. "Man, that kind of stuff gives me the creeps. But we did just get two new titles that are exactly what you're looking for. I haven't had time to unpack them yet; try that bottom box in the corner."

The bell attached to the front door clanged and Al turned to take care of the pretty girl with the tattoo on her neck.

Gil started moving boxes and soon found the books exactly where Al had said they'd be.

CHAPTER 10

THERE WERE MULTIPLE copies of two books in the box, which Gil now remembered he had ordered. Having Claire talk to him about voodoo and Marie Laveau for weeks before they'd left had piqued his interest, causing him to order the books. The first, *Spirits of St. Louis,* covered only that city while the second, *Ghosts Along the Mississippi,* included Tennessee, Mississippi, Illinois and Wisconsin. He was surprised to find there was also a chapter on New Orleans and specifically Marie Laveau. He made a mental note to read about the Voodoo Queen another time, concentrating now on the first chapter, which covered "Clayton's Haunted Condominium"—the very building he and Claire occupied.

Gil brought the books home with him.

Claire took the books away from Gil and began leafing through them while he made tea for her, and coffee for himself. When he came back into the dining room with two cups and cookies, she was engrossed in her reading. "Did you know—" she began, but he cut her off. "Marie Laveau?"

"You read my mind."

"I thought you'd find that chapter."

"Did you read this?"

"Some," he said, "I didn't have time to read it all."

She took a sip of her tea. "It says here that Marie's ghost returns to her home on Saint Anne Street every Halloween."

"Which is about a week away," he said before taking a big bite out of his cookie. "Are you thinking about going back down there?"

"No. I just find all this interesting."

"So do I," he said.

They drank their coffee and tea for a moment and then Gil voiced what was running though his mind.

"You know, Barbara Jedda's husband, Huntley? Maybe he knows something helpful."

"And," Claire said, seizing the thought and putting her own spin on it, "he's Jamaican."

"What does that have to do with anything?"

"Maybe he knows something about voodoo. It did come to America with slaves from the West Indies, and Jamaica is part of those islands. Let's call them to have dinner. It'll give me a chance to get to know Barbara better, too."

"Okay," he said, "so we'll invite our potential good friends to have dinner with us . . ."

"Right."

". . . and then we'll pump them for as much information as we can."

"No," she corrected, "we'll invite a charming couple to dinner in hopes of making new friends. We'll have a wonderful time, and as soon as they're relaxed, know what sincere, caring people we are . . . then we'll pump them for info."

"Sounds like a plan," Gil laughed.

CHAPTER 11

BARBARA AND HUNTLEY accepted the dinner invitation, and arrangements were made to meet several evenings later. While Gil and Claire were dressing, they discussed how and when to bring up their questions.

Claire stood in front of her dresser, trying to choose which earrings to wear. "So you think we'll sound weird asking about voodoo? Scare them off?"

"I don't know. Let's just work as a team tonight, Claire."

"I thought we always did. And if you're going to wear those shoes you have to change your belt."

"I was just going to do that," he grumbled. "As I was saying, it just seems that our goals are a little different at times."

"Goals?" She took a jean jacket out of her closet. "Why don't we just play it by ear?"

"Okay," he said, "but whose?"

The Hunts arrived at Duff's first and were greeted by Karen Duffy, the owner. The personable woman had recently been featured in *St. Louis Magazine* as one of the top businesswomen in the city. Gil knew her because she was a frequent visitor to his store; Claire had met her later at a poetry reading Duff's had sponsored. The restaurant, one of the couple's favorites, was located in the Central West End, and famous for its eclectic menu. Outdoor dining was popular in the spring and summer, but during the fall and winter patrons dined inside the old building with its exposed brick walls, high ceiling and squeaky wooden floors. The various dining rooms had been decorated with mismatched wooden tables and chairs. Candles glowed on the tables and the walls were covered with large canvases painted with warm southwestern colors. A stained-glass window dominated the front of the main dining room.

"You two have been away too long," Karen said, hugging both of them. "Table for two?"

"Four," Gil said. "We're meeting friends."

As she seated them she discussed the newest thriller Gil had recommended. "Well, I'll get Charlie to come take your drink orders. Have a nice evening."

By the time their drinks arrived, so had Barbara and Huntley. As they watched them approach the table, both Gil and Claire were again struck by what an attractive couple they were. Barbara diminutive, lovely and dynamic, Huntley tall, dark and elegantly handsome.

Gil stood and Claire remained seated as they exchanged handshakes and hugs and then all sat around the oblong table. The waiter came to take drink orders from the new arrivals and then left them to peruse the menu.

"This is one of our favorite restaurants," Barbara started the conversation.

"You must come here a lot, living so close," Claire said.

"That's right," Gil said, "I forgot you lived in the area. Over on Maryland, right?"

It didn't take long for the foursome to get comfortable with one another. Through the salad and main course their conversation never slowed down. Huntley talked about his job as a travel consultant and entertained everyone with stories he'd gathered from his encounters with various celebrities. Barbara gushed with pride when the conversation came to her horse, Captain. Gil talked books and Claire admitted she enjoyed her job a bit too much while explaining her duties in front of the camera.

They were on dessert when Claire brought up the subject of New Orleans and voodoo.

"I can't believe you mentioned that." Barbara covered her face with both hands.

Huntley seemed puzzled by his wife's reaction. "Why not?"

"My husband is fascinated with anything supernatural," she said. "The stranger, the better. I don't share his interest."

"Well, I have to admit," Gil said, "I am, too."

Claire took a bite of Gil's ice cream. "The other night he brought home some books all about voodoo. Nothing too scary, just your routine spells and such, but . . ."

"Spirits are nothing to take lightly," Huntley said. "I have seen many unexplainable things where I come from. And I learned to accept those things as truth at a very young age."

"Oh, I'm sorry, I didn't mean to offend you," Claire said.

"It's just that we've been doing some research lately on Marie Laveau . . ."

"Ahh . . ." Huntley slowly nodded his head. "Some say she was the last American witch, that she consorted with

Satan. Growing up in Jamaica, I heard many stories about her even though she lived in America and died more than one hundred years ago."

"She was called the Voodoo Queen," Claire said, still unsure if she had insulted him. "She had beauty, charisma and a whole lot of power. Some believe she even committed murder."

Barbara stirred cream into her coffee. "But I thought voodoo ceremonies were held out in the woods somewhere and nobody ever talked about it. How did she get to be so famous? Wasn't all that stuff supposed to be kept secret?"

"That's why Laveau is still revered today, she mixed up voodooism with Christianity," Gil told her. "She conducted meetings at Bayou Saint John, just outside the city. Crowds of people came—rich, poor. She was said to have been almost saintly to some, gave away all her money to the poor in her neighborhood when times were hard."

"She did that only because it pleased her to do so. No one could force Marie Laveau to do anything. She made powerful gris-gris to help her get what she wanted from people. Money, respect," Huntley said. "She made charms to call up the good or bad luck, selling them to people with money, but mostly using their power for herself."

"We ran into a relative of hers while we were in New Orleans," Claire said.

Now that they were sure they wouldn't frighten their new friends away, Gil and Claire took turns filling Barbara and Huntley in on their trip and how one woman, claiming to be Auntie Laveau, had ended up dead.

"My God!" Barbara said. "That must have been frightening."

"But interesting," Huntley added.

CHAPTER 12

"WHAT IS IT?" Claire put down her copy of Walter Mosley's *Walkin' the Dog* that she was reading to give him her full attention. This was her bedroom book, while her living room book was *Free Love,* by Annette Meyers. The fact that she was reading Mosley meant she was expanding her reading list, usually made up of traditional mysteries. However, she had recently read Mosley's first "Socrates Fortlow" collection, *Always Outnumbered, Always Outgunned,* and then they'd seen Lawrence Fishburne play Fortlow on HBO. So when the new collection came out, Gil had brought it home for her.

"Well, according to this book," Gil said, "she never left New Orleans; in fact, it says she probably never left the Quarter. Can you imagine living your entire life within an area about fifteen by seven blocks? And here we are in Saint Louis decades later, talking about this woman."

Claire groaned. "Sweetie, I'm really sleepy. And I think I've had enough of Marie Laveau for tonight."

She had already burrowed beneath the covers, so he leaned over and kissed her good night.

Over breakfast the next morning Gil continued to talk to Claire about Marie Laveau.

"Were you up all night reading those books?"

"Well . . . I couldn't sleep."

"Then what were you dreaming about?" she asked. "When you finally did come to bed, you were moaning and rolling around."

Sheepishly, he admitted to what he had dreamed. "Gris- gris."

"Oh, fine," she said, rinsing her teacup in the sink. "I hope you're not becoming obsessed with this, Gil. You know how you get sometimes when your interest is piqued."

"I'm not obsessed," he said defensively. "Just interested."

She went into the bedroom to finish getting ready for work.

He got up from the table to go pour himself another cup of coffee, then put her cup and both their plates in the dishwasher. When she reappeared she was looking smart in a new outfit.

"New designer?" he asked.

"You noticed," she said, kissing him.

He walked her to the door. When she left he took his coffee into the office they shared and sat down at his computer.

"Obsessed," he mumbled to himself. "Just show a little enthusiasm and all of a sudden I'm obsessed." He swiveled his chair around to face a small shelf and stacked the books he had brought home for research in a neat pile on top. Just as he was settling in, getting ready to go online, the phone rang, startling him.

"Mr. Hunt?" a man's voice asked after he said hello.

"Yes, that's right. Who's this?" He was hoping it wasn't a telemarketer.

"Mr. Hunt, this is Detective LaSalle, from New Orleans. Remember?"

"Of course I remember, Detective. How are you?"

"Very well, sir," LaSalle said, "but I do need your help."

"In what way?"

"I would appreciate it if you or your wife could come back down here, if that's possible."

"Why?"

"We have a woman in the hospital I'd like one of you to take a look at, see if you can identify her."

"Identify her as . . . who?"

"I'd like to know if she's the woman you and your wife had your meeting with at the cemetery."

"What happened? Why is she in the hospital?"

"We're not sure," LaSalle said. "At the moment she's in a coma. She has a head injury. Apparently someone attacked her."

"That's terrible," Gil said. "How serious is it?"

"She might come out of it—she might not."

"So . . . by the time I get there I might be identifying . . . a dead body?" Gil asked.

"It's possible."

Gil hesitated a moment before saying, "Claire's busy with her job and won't be able to get the time off, so I guess I'll be coming alone."

"You own your own business, if I remember correctly, Mr. Hunt?"

"Yes, a bookstore."

"Ahh, then, since you're the boss, I guess it's easy to give yourself some time off. I hate to rush you, sir, but we'd appreciate it if you could fly down as soon as possible," LaSalle said. "If you could get here before she . . . while she's still alive, it would be better for all of us."

"I'll try to get a flight out in the morning."

"The ticket will be expensive," LaSalle said. "The city will reimburse you."

"Oh well . . . that's very decent of the city. Thank you."

"You will, uh, have to pay for your own hotel, I'm afraid," LaSalle said apologetically.

"That's fine," Gil said. "Don't worry about it."

"This is very decent of you, sir."

"Well, we did tell you we wanted to help."

"People tell me a lot of things, in my line of work, that they don't mean. So, I thank you for your integrity," LaSalle said.

Gil was impressed with the man's frankness. "Where should I meet you?"

"If you'll call me after you've booked your flight, I'll be happy to pick you up at the airport."

"Okay," Gil said. "I'll give you a call."

"Here's my cell-phone number," LaSalle said, "in case I'm not in my office."

Gil wrote it down.

"Again, Mr. Hunt, I appreciate this."

"No problem, Detective," Gil said. "I'll talk to you later."

Gil hung up, not sure how he felt about the turn of events. All this research on Marie Laveau, and now he was being called back to New Orleans. Odd, but fortuitous. At least he'd be able to hit the bookstores this time. He wondered how Claire was going to react. She was still on the air, so he couldn't talk to her now. He was about to pick up the phone to call the airlines when it rang again. "Hello?"

"Gil? It's Huntley."

"Hey, how are you?"

"Fine," he said, "just fine. And Claire?"

They went through the polite ritual before Huntley got to the point of his call.

"I'm leaving on a trip today," he said, "but I told a friend of mine about you and he wanted me to ask if you appraise book collections."

"As a matter of fact, I do," Gil said.

"That's wonderful. He has a collection and no idea what it's worth. Apparently he inherited it. He said he would pay your fee and also your travel and hotel expenses."

"That's very generous," Gil said. "I have to leave town tomorrow, but when I get back I'll get in touch with him."

"Excellent. I'm off to Puerto Rico. Where are you headed?"

"Back to New Orleans, I'm afraid," Gil said. "The police need me down there to help identify someone."

There was a long silence on Huntley's end.

"Is something wrong?" Gil asked.

"Remember our conversation the other night? I told you how I believe that what appears to be a coincidence is just fate pointing the way?"

"Of course I do, I've thought about that quite a lot," Gil said.

"Well, my friend lives in Shreveport. You might be able to defray some of the cost of your trip if you combine the two."

"I suppose I could," Gil agreed, not bothering to mention that the city of New Orleans would be footing the bill for his airfare. "Still, when things fall into place like this, I'm always somewhat leery."

Huntley laughed. "Oh, no, my friend, you must feel comforted knowing there is a grand plan."

"I suppose so."

"In any case, I will give you my friend's phone number. You can call him when you get a chance."

"Shoot." Gil picked up a pen and wrote the number beneath Detective LaSalle's.

After saying their good-byes, they hung up. Gil snatched up the phone before it could ring again and dialed TWA.

"So you're going to New Orleans without me?" Claire asked.

They were walking to Café Napoli, one of their favorite places. Claire had gotten home late, having had to fill in for one of the other hosts that evening.

"Yes," Gil said, "unless you can get the next few days off."

"Few days?"

Gil zipped up his jacket; the air had turned chilly that day. "Well, there's no point in me flying down there, taking a look at this old woman, and flying right back," he said. "That would be a waste of time and money, wouldn't it?"

She pushed her hands deep into the pockets of her heavy cardigan. "You're justifying."

"Hey, if you can get the time off . . ."

"I can't. Driving to New Orleans cost me some vacation time."

"I know."

"What about Huntley's friend?"

"I called him," Gil said. "If I can get over to Shreveport, I'll make a healthy profit on the trip."

"Well, I guess that's the good part."

"Come on," he said, reaching for her hand, "it'll only be a few days."

"If you can stand it, I guess I can."

He smiled. "It'll be torture."

"Right answer, bucko."

CHAPTER 13

THE NEW ORLEANS International Airport was located in Kenner, Louisiana, about fifteen miles from New Orleans. When Gil deplaned, Detective LaSalle was right there waiting for him.

After the two men shook hands, LaSalle asked, "Do you have any luggage to claim?"

"No," Gil said, lifting his two-suiter carry-on in one hand and a small green bag in the other, "just these."

"Let me help you," LaSalle said, taking the green bag from him. "This way out."

Gil walked alongside the detective as the man guided them through the terminal. Having caught a 6-A.M. flight out of Saint Louis' Lambert Airport, he felt as though he hadn't quite woken up yet.

"How is she doing?" Gil finally asked.

"Better," LaSalle said. "She's off the critical list, but they don't know when—if ever—she'll come out of the coma."

Gil walked along with LaSalle through the main hall of the terminal, past the Lucky Dog stand and a Dixieland band. Glancing up, his eyes caught sight of the jazz greats captured in giant murals on the walls. Being with the detective felt odd, as if he had come to visit a long-lost relative. It was awkward and neither had very much to say to the other. He decided to keep silent as long as the detective did, since he was the visitor and LaSalle was the host. Let the policeman carry the conversation if there was to be one at all.

In the car LaSalle spoke long enough to tell Gil that the woman was in Physicians Hospital on Canal Street, five minutes from the Bourbon Orleans Hotel—where Gil had told him on the phone the previous night that he'd booked a room.

"Would you like to stop at your hotel first and freshen up?"

"No, that's okay," Gil said. "Don't we have to be there during visiting hours?"

"You forget—I'm the police. For me it's always visiting hours."

"I never thought of that," Gil said mostly to himself. "Thanks anyway, but I'm fine; let's go straight to the hospital."

"Sure thing."

And that was it for conversation.

Gil was actually grateful for the lack of small talk. The men soon fell into a kind of easy silence during the ride and by the time they reached the hospital were more comfortable with each other.

"Yes, Detective," the nurse at the front desk said, "you may go in, but please don't stay long."

"Why?" he asked. "Is she having visitors?"

"No, but—"

"Will we tire her out?"

"I uh—"

"Get me the doctor," he said, and then turned to Gil. "Come on."

He led the way down the hall to an elevator.

"You were pretty tough on her," Gil said, while they were going up.

"Was I?" LaSalle asked roughly, and then, in a calmer tone, added, "Maybe so. It's just that . . . I hate hospitals. They make me uneasy."

"Oh."

"My mother was in one for . . . well, a long time before she died. To this day I think she would have lived longer—or at least better—at home."

"That's a shame."

LaSalle clasped his hands tightly in front of him. "Yeah, well, if my son-of-a-bitch father hadn't left us, we could have afforded home care and . . . it was a long time ago."

Gil remained quiet. Silence was better than the tension he felt from LaSalle's anger.

They got out of the elevator and the detective led the way to the woman's room.

"What's her name?" Gil asked.

"We don't know. We ran her prints but apparently she's never been arrested, and never been printed."

"No personal effects?"

"None."

"Was she robbed?"

"That's what it looks like."

"Then why—"

"Later," LaSalle said, as they entered the room.

The woman had gray hair and a pallor to match. She looked incredibly small in the hospital bed. Stiff white sheets were pulled up to her neck. An IV dripped down a long tube and into her arm. A heart monitor beeped regularly.

"Now, please take a good look at her, Mr. Hunt. Tell me if you've ever seen this woman before."

Gil leaned forward. "All right." He studied the frail patient, wanting to be absolutely sure. But it didn't take him more than a minute. "That's her."

"That's who?" LaSalle asked. "Can you be more specific for me?"

"This is the woman my wife and I met in the cemetery."

"The woman who gave you the Mardi Gras mask?"

"Yes."

LaSalle came closer to the bed and looked down at the patient lying there. "Are you sure?"

"Yes."

"All right."

"If she has no identification," Gil asked, "and no effects, how did you find her here?"

"She had this on her when she was brought in." LaSalle handed Gil something across the bed.

"It's my business card."

"Look on the back."

Gil turned it over and saw the name "Kelly Denoux" written in pencil.

"When the case came across my desk I recognized both names," LaSalle said.

"It's the same name that was on the back of the mask."

"Correct, sir."

Gil watched the old woman. A large bandage covered

most of her forehead. He suddenly felt so sorry for her. "Detective LaSalle?"

Both Gil and LaSalle turned to see a doctor standing in the doorway.

"Excuse me a minute, Mr. Hunt," LaSalle said.

"Sure."

The detective went to the door and stepped into the hall to talk to the doctor.

Gil looked down at his business card. It said: THE DELMAR BOOK SHOP on it in bold maroon letters. Beneath that: *Gil Hunt* and beneath that: *New & Used, Fiction, Nonfiction* and then, in one corner: *Appraisals*. In addition there was the address and phone number of the store. He now had e-mail, didn't have it when he first got the cards made up. Claire told him once that they were the busiest business cards she'd ever seen.

"What happened to you?" he asked the comatose woman.

At the exact moment he turned his head to look at the door, someone grabbed his wrist in a viselike grip. Startled, he looked down and saw the old woman's hand clamped on to him. Her eyes were open, wide and staring up at her visitor.

"You came," she said.

CHAPTER 14

A GLOSSY PICTURE of Saint Michael was tacked above the altar. She had been taught to believe in his ability to help conquer her enemies. Now she called on him for help once again. Small mirrors reflected the many candles that burned in the darkness of the room. Another bright morning was in full bloom outside, but within her walls, it was always night.

A large amulet in the shape of a snake swung from the woman's neck as she slowly undressed. Quickly she mumbled a prayer to herself while rubbing her skin down with grass oil. When that was finished, she stepped into her new caftan. Wearing a piece of new clothing for the first time on a Wednesday was a good omen; anything she initiated today would succeed. After wrapping her long hair in a brightly colored strip of fabric to match her dress, she slipped into a pair of worn black sandals.

The bottle of wormwood oil was on the altar next to her Bible. She grabbed it and rushed out the front door. Not caring if anyone saw her, she sprinkled the substance around the foundation of her house. A rosebush snagged her but she was too involved to notice or care about the scratches it left on her thick ankles.

When she was finished circling the house, she ran back through the door she had exited. Racing into the kitchen, she yanked open a small drawer and rummaged through the clutter for a tablet of paper. Taking it over to the table, she picked up the pen she used to do her crossword puzzles.

Her glasses were on the counter behind her and she reached for them without turning. Once she had everything she needed, she concentrated on making the letters clean and bold. Seven times she wrote the name. Holding the paper out at arm's length, she lifted her glasses and admired her neatness. Ripping the sheet from the pad, she folded the scrap into a small square and tucked it into her pocket.

She grabbed a fringed shawl but didn't bother to lock her door when she left. Neighbors knew enough to leave her alone. As she headed down toward the Square, she smiled at Leonce, who stood on the corner strumming a guitar for the tourists.

"Morning, MaMa," he said.

"Morning, child." Her voice was deep.

"And where would you be off to in such a hurry?"

She stopped a moment, causing his fingers to freeze above the strings. "I don't t'ink it's a wise ting for you to be stickin' dat nose of yours in me business today. Are you understandin' what I be tellin' you? Answer me, boy."

Even though Leonce was forty-five, he stared down at the sidewalk as if he were a three-year-old. "Yes, ma'am."

Clutching the shawl around her beefy arms, she continued on her way.

The driver was used to seeing the large black woman in this part of the Quarter. And he also knew by the determination of her gait that he should avoid making eye contact.

But when she stopped in front of his horse, he couldn't help watching out of the corner of his eye.

Taking the paper from her pocket, she shoved it into the mouth of the horse that was hitched up to the buggy. Then she quickly ran away, never looking back.

The horse chewed on the scrap for a moment before spitting it out. His driver knew the woman was an odd one, but he had never seen her do anything like that before. Rushing to the front of his animal, the man bent to pick up the soggy piece of paper. Unfolding it, he wondered who GIL HUNT was and why his name had been written over and over.

CHAPTER 15

"THE DOCTOR SAID she was still in a coma," Detective LaSalle said.

"And I'm telling you she opened her eyes, looked at me, grabbed my wrist and said, 'You came.'"

They were back in LaSalle's car; he was driving Gil to his hotel.

"Okay," LaSalle said, "let's say, for the sake of argument—"

"For the sake of argument?"

"—that what you think happened is true. Why would she say that to you?"

"I don't know."

"How could she come out of a coma long enough to talk to you and then fall right back into unconsciousness?"

Gil shrugged. "I don't know that, either."

"And if she did that, if she managed to speak to you, how then could she fool the doctor after he examined her again? How could she make him think she was still in a coma?"

"I . . . don't. . . know," Gil said, trying to control his temper. "Now you answer one for me."

"Go ahead."

"Why would I come all this way to lie to you?"

LaSalle didn't speak right away, then said, "Well, I guess you wouldn't."

"Then you believe me?"

LaSalle looked at him quickly, then back at the road. "I guess I pretty much have to, don't I?" he said finally. "After all, I'm the one who brought you here."

"That's right," Gil said, reaching into the pocket of his leather jacket. "By the way, here's my ticket stub. Cost me an arm and a leg to get a flight with no advance booking."

LaSalle took it and tucked it under the visor in the car. "I'll have it taken care of."

"Thank you."

LaSalle tried changing his tone to sound friendlier. He was feeling a bit guilty about treating his passenger so curtly. "Will you be going back tomorrow?" he asked.

"No. The last time we were here, we decided to cut our sightseeing short and I never got to the bookstores in the Quarter."

"That's right, you're in the book business."

"I also have a job to do in Shreveport."

"What kind of job?"

"I examine book collections and appraise their value so they can be insured or sold."

"And you get paid for that?"

Gil was finding this man harder and harder to like. "It's part of what I do," he said stiffly.

"I'm sorry," LaSalle said, "no offense; it's just that books are such a small part of my life."

Gil always felt that kind of remark came from people

who were unwittingly admitting to their own ignorance, but he'd spent enough time with LaSalle to know he was anything but ignorant.

They rode the rest of the way in silence, each alone with his thoughts. Gil was thinking about the woman in the hospital. He could still feel the cold grip she'd had on his wrist. He looked at LaSalle, wondered what was running through the detective's mind. Was he sorry he'd asked him to come identify the woman? Had the incident in the hospital room suddenly made his job—and his life—more complicated?

When LaSalle pulled up in front of the Bourbon Orleans Hotel, he hopped out to get Gil's luggage from the trunk.

"Could you do me a favor?" Gil asked, accepting the bags.

"What?"

"While I'm here, if that woman wakes up, will you let me know?"

"Sure," LaSalle said, straightening his shoulders, "why not? Considering what you say happened, you'll probably be the first one she asks for."

"Thanks."

"Is this where you stayed last time?" the detective asked curiously, walking back to the driver's side of the car.

"No, why?"

"It's just odd that you would pick this hotel."

"Why?"

LaSalle opened his door. "It's supposed to be haunted."

CHAPTER 16

"YOU HAVE GOT TO BE KIDDING!" Claire said. "Is there one spot left in the world that isn't haunted by some disgruntled ghost hanging on to his old homestead for dear life?"

Gil laughed at his wife's unintentional joke. "Hey, don't get so excited. I didn't say I believed him. Besides, our friend the detective seems to be the type of person who only believes in what he can see with his own two bloodshot eyes."

"So you think he drinks?"

"No," Gil said. "I think he works a lot of hours and doesn't get very much sleep."

Claire wrapped a fleece throw around her legs. In addition to the damp chill threatening the city with sleet, the idea of her home as well as her husband's hotel being haunted caused her to shiver uncontrollably. "And this whole thing about the old lady grabbing your arm in the hospital is too weird. I feel as though we're living in some old horror movie."

"Well, if Bela Lugosi shows up, I'll let you know."

"Don't make fun of this, Gil. What if that woman's coma is the first stage of her being turned into a zombie? You're in voodoo country, my love; it could happen, you know."

"Claire, in order for someone to be brought back to life as a zombie, they have to die first."

"Well, it's all giving me the creeps. When are you coming home?" she asked.

"I'm due in Shreveport by the weekend. I figure that job shouldn't last more than a few days, which'll put me back home in about a week." He could keep the store closed till then. The money for evaluating the collection would make up for it.

"Good. I miss you."

Gil kicked his shoes off his feet. "I miss you, too. So, what's new there? Anything exciting going on at the station?" he asked as he stretched out on the king-size bed.

"Oh, Ben's all gung ho about changing the format again. For someone rich and smart enough to own a television station, he can sure get real dumb."

"So are you mad at all men today, or just Ben in particular?"

Claire was amazed at his perception. It had taken a few years for Gil to pick up on her signals, but now he was an expert at reading her. "Today . . . I'm mad at all of you. I don't want you to be miles away from me. I wish that Huntley wouldn't have mentioned anything about our condo being haunted because now I see things flitting around out of the corner of my eye and I don't like being afraid. I'm mad at Detective LaSalle for doubting your story and I'm mad at the guy who killed that Auntie Laveau woman in the first place."

"What makes you think a man killed her?"

"Humm, I don't know."

A knock came at Gil's door. He shouted across the room, "Just a minute."

"Who's that?" Claire asked.

"My dinner."

"Go get it; I'll wait."

Gil laid the phone down on the velvet bedspread and hurried to the door.

"Room service," the handsome waiter announced. Where shall I put this, sir?" He stood behind a cart covered with a white linen tablecloth. Several items were laid out on china plates, covered with silver metal lids.

"Over there." Gil pointed to the sitting area.

After he had signed the bill and the waiter had gone, Gil returned to the bed and picked up the receiver. "I'm starving, hon, and more tired than I've been in a long time."

"Go eat, then."

"I'll talk to you tomorrow."

"Okay. And, Gil?"

"Yeah?"

"Please . . . please be careful."

CHAPTER 17

THE FAULKNER HOUSE in Pirate's Alley was known as "America's most charming bookstore," and had been at the top of Gil's list of places to go for years. He had planned to visit the national literary landmark many times, but other things in his life had always planted detours. Today, however, nothing could stop him from relishing every delicious moment. He would spend the entire day exploring bookstores throughout the Quarter. And should he start feeling guilty, he could always convince himself that he was really working, researching.

Using Saint Louis Cathedral as a starting point, Gil walked around to the rear garden, down the alley, to number 624. Through research, he had found out that William Faulkner had subleased the ground floor from William Spratling, a famous artist, designer and architect, in 1925. It was from this site Faulkner had written his first novel, *Soldiers' Pay*, as well as fallen in love and been inspired to write a series of poetic sketches.

As Gil opened the front door, a bell suspended over the

entrance signaled his presence to the woman seated at the large table in the middle of the room.

She looked up from the book she was reading. "Hello, can I help you?"

"No, I'm just going to look around, thanks."

Gil started with the books displayed nearest the front door; they featured the life and works of William Faulkner as well as local history. As he walked across the wooden floor, it creaked beneath his feet. The rooms housing the bookstore smelled of old paper and the fragrance immediately took him back to his childhood.

On weekends, his parents would drive from Brooklyn into Manhattan for a day of shopping at Macy's department store. The trip was filled with such anticipation, it made his heart quicken, and as he rode the escalator up he had to hold on tight or he would have run full power to the book department. It was his earliest recollection of a specific activity being experienced through every one of his senses.

Oh, the smells. Paper and ink and dust. Touching all those pulpy magazines, running his fingers over slick, glossy covers. Colors! A sexy blonde dressed in a red nightgown, holding a pewter-colored gun over the body of her husband, who lay dead on the floor. Vibrant blues and yellows drawn inside panels of a *Superman* comic. Mystery, suspense, horror, science fiction. Paperbacks, heavy beautiful hardcovers, thin soft comic books. And then finally getting to buy the book he had so carefully chosen. Waiting in line with his allowance gripped in his hands. Listening to the clerk ring up sale after sale, he could almost taste the joy.

And today, in the middle of this store, he could feel it all stirring inside him again.

The manager came up behind him, offering again to help. He didn't want to appear rude, but he could find his way around the shelves without any assistance. Besides, he wanted to be left alone to explore. Politely, he reassured her he'd ask if he needed anything. She smiled and went back to her table.

There was a section featuring local authors and Gil passed the familiar titles written by Julie Smith, Ann Rice, Tony Fennelly and James Lee Burke. He looked at everything, losing and enjoying himself for close to an hour. He thought how Claire would have gone next door for a cold drink long before now. She appreciated his interest in books but couldn't quite match his stamina when it came to the hunt.

After making a complete circle around the room, he was back where he started when he noticed a book on a bottom shelf. *The French Quarter: An Informal History of the New Orleans Underworld,* by Herbert Asbury. Leafing through a few pages, Gil noticed the copyright date was 1936. The pages were yellowed; he brought it closer to his nose and inhaled the age. He had seen this book featured on the Internet and debated whether or not to buy it before deciding against the purchase. But now, actually holding it in his hands, he was changing his mind, realizing this was what he had given up shopping by computer. Reading down the table of contents, he noticed the first few chapters dealt with the river, gambling and filibusters, but chapter 9 was all about voodoo. It seemed to be a sign and Gil tucked it under his arm, telling himself this book would not only serve as a good research source but also be a souvenir of his trip.

"Will there be anything else?" the timid woman asked when Gil walked over to check out.

"Yes, I was wondering if it would be possible to see the rest of the house?"

"I'm sorry, but you'd have to make an appointment. There are private living quarters upstairs. But I could call . . ."

"Oh, no," Gil said "It was just a thought. Please, don't trouble yourself."

The woman began writing up a receipt. "How long will you be visiting New Orleans?"

"Is it that obvious I'm a tourist?" Gil asked.

"I just detected a slight Brooklyn accent . . . very slight." She kept her eyes on her work.

"Well, I was born and raised there, but now I live in Saint Louis."

"Really?" She looked at him and he could see her blue eyes light up. "My sister lives in South County."

That did it; Gil had made himself a new friend. They talked about bookstores all across the Midwest, weather, food and family. He was wondering how to retreat without seeming rude when another customer walked into the store. The woman apologized for having to wind down their conversation. Gil thanked her and started to turn toward the door when she stopped him.

"Maybe you could use this," she said, handing him a map of all the antiquarian and secondhand bookshops in New Orleans.

Another sign, life was full of them today, he thought. "Thanks so much, this is great."

After finally leaving the store, Gil walked to Jackson Square. Smelling the hot dogs being sold by a nearby vendor, he realized he was hungry. A band was playing in front of the Cathedral and he stopped to listen, amazed at the fact that everyone in the city seemed to move to the rhythm of some music they could feel clear and even, down to their soles. They all walked with such elegance and grace, almost gliding across the pavement. Suddenly he felt so out of place.

He strolled down Chartres Street toward the closest store marked on his map: Librairie Books. It was warm inside, a large glass case stood to the left of the door and he was again struck by the delightful aromas and sounds. He would have liked to stay longer, but after half an hour he couldn't ignore the growling in his stomach.

Standing in front of the shop, he was blinded by the brilliant afternoon sun and dug in his pocket for sunglasses. He began walking quickly down Saint Ann, toward Bourbon Street, thinking about having étouffée for lunch. Before he folded the small map into his pocket, he glanced at it once more. Maybe if he hadn't been distracted, he would have noticed the large woman standing in the doorway watching him.

CHAPTER 18

DETECTIVE LASALLE DECIDED to take the ferry to Algiers, hoping the slow steady ride would give him insight. He needed a new perspective on the crime that had gone unsolved for more than two weeks. As he sat inside the large boat on a molded plastic seat, he couldn't help but notice a young couple passionately kissing. Instead of being annoyed at the loud sucking sounds they made, he envied them.

The ride took a little over fifteen minutes. As the boat docked, he could see the warehouse famous for manufacturing Mardi Gras floats, one of the few tourist attractions in this area. He disembarked, walking down the planked incline. Gravel crunched beneath his shoes, dust coated the shiny leather.

There were only a dozen or so people in the tight group moving toward the parking lot. Several got into waiting cars. By the time he had passed the local bar, he was the only one walking in the residential area.

As he neared the small A-frame, he could see yellow police tape on the front door flapping in the warm breeze. LaSalle used the key he had gotten from the property room at the station, and after unlocking the weathered door, stepped over a plastic strip secured across the frame.

The murder scene had been gone over by his men, the medical examiner's team, as well as forensics. It had been photographed and scrutinized from every possible angle. Walking toward the back room, where the body had been found, he wondered why no one had come forward to claim the house yet, let alone make arrangements to bury the body of Auntie Laveau . . . or whoever she was. No relatives, no clues. He shook his head.

It was chilly inside out of the sun, and he shoved his hands deep into the pockets of his sports coat. White tape that had outlined the body was still intact, as were black puddles of dried blood. He stopped, heaving a sigh, and was suddenly more aware of the absolute silence shrouding the house.

This was his third visit. The first time had been sparked with the usual commotion. The second had been calmer, but still involved too many others. This time he had come alone, purposefully, to sniff the air without any interruptions.

He stared at the bloodied floor, then at a small table in the corner and watched dust settling over it. There wasn't much furniture in the room—just two old chairs and the table topped with an ornate brass lamp. He stood and listened.

Nothing.

With his hands still buried in his pockets, LaSalle walked to the kitchen and gave it a quick once-over. A calendar, one of those large ones with a generic woodland scene and the name of an insurance agent in large black letters across the top, covered a three-foot square on the wall opposite the sink. He was starting to turn, to go check out the bedroom when he noticed that the corner of the October page flapped. Stopping short, he cocked his head, waiting, trying to feel air circulating through the room. When the pages fluttered again, he walked over to inspect the wall, thinking it odd that the calendar had been positioned so low.

The whole thing had been secured by one large nail. When he pulled it free, he discovered a keyhole. Painted the same shade of navy blue as the room, the door had easily blended into the wall. He was about to look for a key when he accidentally leaned against the door and it clicked open.

There was a light switch on the wall, to the right. After flipping it up, he could see a wooden staircase leading down into a basement. Removing his gun from the holster inside his jacket, he held it in front of him as he descended into the chilly room.

LaSalle could move his six-foot frame easily around the room without having to bend or stoop. He walked into the middle of the dirt floor. A single bulb dangled from a frayed cord, illuminating most of the area but leaving all four corners in shadow. He looked around for another source of light. A window, ground level, had been covered over with black paper. He ripped it free of the nails securing it to the stone wall. Sunlight streamed inside, brightening up the dingy hole.

Confident he was alone, he returned his gun to its holster, freeing up both hands. Silence rang in his ears and he sniffed, sure he could smell something spoiled. LaSalle stood frozen, wondering at the total absence of furniture, and the clutter people invariably seemed to accumulate throughout a lifetime.

Walking slowly into the center of the room he squinted at the floor, making out the indentation of a perfect square all around him. He looked up. A heavy chain hung from a wooden beam.

Now that his eyes had fully adjusted, he could see several other windows, each covered with the same heavy paper, and as he walked around the room, clearing the panes, he wondered, Why? What had this peculiar room been used for?

He ended up facing the underside of the wooden staircase. The bright light now flooding into the room enabled him to make out a small door built under the stairs. It looked to be a storage space of some sort. The warped door was held tight with a piece of rusted wire which he easily unwound. Before he had a chance to open the door, it flew open on its own. Startled, he jumped back.

A cardboard box lay at his feet, its contents scattered all around him. Kneeling down, he examined candles of all shapes and colors, amulets, beads and a small drum. LaSalle's experience on the force, especially in the New Orleans area, had educated him enough to know he was looking at ritual paraphernalia used to adorn an altar in voodoo ceremonies. Poking his head inside the crawl space, he found a large chunk of rock had been propped against the back wall. He recognized it as what locals called a "pe," or altar stone.

He kept telling himself he should have brought a flashlight, but it was in his car on the other side of the river. LaSalle dragged another box out into the light and lifted the lid to find pieces of broken china. Digging inside it, he came up with a handful of colorful shards. He brought them closer, trying to figure out exactly what he was looking at, when something hit his shoe and skidded into a corner.

Replacing the china in the box, then brushing dust from his hands, he went to retrieve the object on the floor. It was roughly the size of a half-dollar and appeared to be a Mardi Gras mask. Turning it over, he was surprised to see the name "Kelly Denoux" written in black. The same name that had been on the mask he had gotten from the Hunts. Making a mental note to run a check on it when he got back to his office, he carefully wrapped the mask in his handkerchief, burying it deep in his pocket.

He straightened up, surveyed the room once again, scanning the rough stone walls. A flash of white caught his eye, something was sticking out of a small crack in the wall opposite him. He walked across the room, careful not to disturb the large square indentation in the floor.

Tugging at the piece of paper, he could see it had been ripped from a ruled pad. It was small and he had to walk closer to the window to read it. In pencil was scrawled, *I'm still alive,* signed by Kelly Denoux.

The detective leaned against the wall, resting his cheek along the cool rough surface. From that vantage point he was able to see them, like brisdes on a brush, dozens of points of paper stuck between the stones. Row after row that couldn't have been seen if the windows were still covered.

He pulled several loose and read:

"Help!

"THEY'RE GOING TO KILL ME!

"KELLY DENOUX."

CHAPTER 19

AFTER TWO DAYS OF "BOOKING" through the Quarter, Gil was feeling a little guilty. He was having far too much fun to consider his exploring real work. And after talking with Claire the night before, hearing that Saint Louis was suffering through a bout of icy rain, he felt even guiltier enjoying the sunny, warm afternoon. Hoping to unburden himself, he walked down Royal Street in search of a gift for his wife.

ACCENTS "Shopping for the Unique." The sign beckoned him into the small shop. Looking around, he couldn't help but mumble to himself, "Perfect."

"Can I help you?" an attractive woman sitting behind a low counter in the back asked. She was close to his age, with a curly mass of long black hair. Bent over a box of necklaces, she was trying to untangle the delicate gold and silver chains.

"I hope so," Gil said, slowly making his way toward her.

A young couple were trying bracelets on each other, giggling. They never even turned to check out the new arrival.

"I'm looking for a present for my wife."

The woman peered above her glasses, revealing big brown eyes. "Have a fight?"

Gil laughed. "No, no, nothing like that."

The woman swept her long curly hair across her forehead. "Don't tell me, let me guess then."

"But—"

"I'm having a really bad day," the woman said. "Let me have some fun. Please . . . I need this."

Gil crossed his arms, willing to play. "Okay. Go for it." He stood back and waited.

"You have honest eyes, so I bet you suck at lying. You'd never get away with cheating on your wife."

"Probably not." Gil grinned.

"Judging from your age—no offense—"

"—None taken—"

"And the fact that you're in my pricey little shop, I'd guess that the wife you're buying something for is your second."

"How'd you know that?"

"The first wife usually has to struggle through the poor years. Small appliances and zircons for Christmas. Then you guys have to strut. For a few years, it's diamonds—small ones—and fancy cars. Have to impress the boss, you know. But you settle in, adjust, mature. And just when it looks like a real life is going to happen—BAM—you dump us and spend all your cash on the new lady."

"Well . . . not exactly."

"I think I'm also safe in assuming you're a tourist. The map sticking out of your pocket is a tip-off on that one."

"Right."

"So, I ask myself, what kind of man travels without his wife and feels that it's necessary to bring home a gift? Either one who has to be forgiven for something or one who just plain misses his better half."

"Definitely the second scenario," Gil said. "Now it's my turn. May I?"

"Be my guest." She smiled, sitting up straight on the tall stool behind her counter.

"You married your childhood sweetheart, probably the boy who lived a few houses down from yours in the old neighborhood. Had a big church wedding, worked hard, put your career plans on hold. You helped him through school, sacrificed, everything you did was for him. You were selfless, single-minded. Then, out of nowhere, he took off with his secretary."

She blushed. "God, it's so corny but truer than hell."

"You're divorced with two children . . . both are away at school in . . ."

"California. One's at UCLA the other's at Berkeley."

"You have a great relationship with them but hope neither will get married before they're thirty."

"You're good," the woman laughed. "Real good. You should set up a table in Jackson Square."

"Just old enough to have met a lot of angry exes," Gil told her.

"Sorry if I came off so bitter." She held out her hand. "I'm Nadine."

"Gil." He shook her hand. "We all have bad days. I run my own business, too. I know how it is."

"So, Gil, now that we've psychoanalyzed each other, tell me what your wife likes . . . besides you."

Gil hesitated a moment. Claire was always telling him how women flirted with him but he usually thought she was kidding. Now he was beginning to think maybe she wasn't the only female who found him irresistible—or, at least, likable.

"My wife has a high-profile job; she's elegant, funny, and loves jewelry of any kind. She has boxes of it stashed all over our bedroom. She can't seem to get enough."

"A lady after my own heart. What's her birthstone?"

"Sapphire. But I was looking for something special. Something you could only get in New Orleans."

Nadine snapped her fingers and Gil could see she had a ring on every finger. "I know just the thing. They came in today. Stay right there."

"I won't move."

Nadine lifted a beaded shawl draped across an archway and opened the door behind it. She disappeared into a back room. Gil leaned over to inspect the bracelets laid out in the glass case in front of him. There were gems of every color, set in silver and gold, a few in copper. Each had a small card next to it with the artist's name. Claire would love this place, he thought to himself.

The shop smelled of vanilla and he turned around as the young couple exited through the front door, slamming it shut behind them. His eyes scanned the wall nearest the display window. It was covered with necklaces draped over small pegs. Every item he looked at seemed more enticing than the next.

"Here we go," Nadine said as she set a tray of rings on the counter. "If you don't find something here your wife would love, she has to be from Mars."

"Claire's one of a kind, that's for sure, but I'm positive she's from this planet."

"Good, then you can't go wrong with any one of these." Nadine picked up a ruby ring and handed it to Gil. "This is one of my favorites. The artist does this style with all kinds of gemstones. She lives just around the comer. You won't find anything like it anywhere else. Promise."

Gil took the ring. Intrigued by the way the gold had been wrapped around the stone in delicate twists, he knew it would look perfect on Claire's slender finger. "It's great! She'll love it; I'll take it."

"Wait a minute. You haven't looked at any of the others. They're all different."

"Exactly," Gil said. "If I look, I'll get tempted and soon won't be able to make any kind of decision."

"I bet you put off your Christmas shopping until the day before."

"It's the best time to go. The sales are great and the selection is limited . . ."

". . . making it easier to choose. I get it."

"You know, the older I get, the easier I try to make things on myself."

"I should try that," Nadine said while she gift-wrapped the ring. "When I get old, that is."

Gil watched the woman tie a small bow on the bright wrapping paper. Reaching into his pocket for his wallet, he happened to glance down at a bottom shelf near his right foot. Among the beaded evening bags was a small Mardi Gras mask. Bending down, he picked it up.

It was the same size as the one Claire had received from Auntie Laveau, only these eyes had been set with tiny green stones. The whole thing was mounted on top of a gold disk with a chain strung through the metal loop on the back.

"This is pretty," he said.

"The college girls love 'em; I can't keep them on the shelves when the kids hit here for spring break."

"Is this the only one you have?"

"Right now? Yeah. I have to get a new supplier."

"Why?" Gil asked.

"The woman I've been buying from died, suddenly."

"Auntie Laveau?"

"Oh, you read about it in the paper?" Nadine asked, handing him the package. "Such a shame, she was a nice lady."

"How much is this?" Gil asked, holding the mask up.

"Fifteen dollars, but because you're such a good customer"—she smiled—"how about ten?"

"Sounds fair."

Gil paid the bill with his credit card and when Nadine started to put the mask in the bag with the ring, he stopped her. "Can I borrow your scissors, please?" he asked, pointing.

Confused, the woman shrugged. "Sure."

With the sharp edge, Gil pried the backing off the mask. There it was, written in black: KELLY DENOUX.

Nadine could see his surprise. "What's wrong?"

Gil held up the mask. "Do you know this woman?"

She leaned across the counter to glance at the name and he could smell her hair. It reminded him that he hadn't been close to Claire in days.

"Kelly? I've met her."

"You have?" he asked, excited. "What do you know about her?"

"Not much," Nadine said, leaning back. "She's young, works . . . worked . . . for Auntie Laveau. That wasn't her real name, you know. There are so many women in this town who think they're descended from Marie Laveau—"

"I'm beginning to see that," he said. "But about Kelly . . ."

"Do you know her?"

"Not at all, but I've come across the name before and I was curious. Have you seen her lately?"

"Come to think of it, no," she said.

"Did she deliver the orders to you?"

"Sometimes she did, sometimes this older woman, sometimes a young man. Auntie had lots of people working for her."

"Do you think she was involved with voodoo?"

"With that name? I'd bet on it."

He dropped the mask into the bag with Claire's gift. "Well, Nadine, thanks very much for all your help."

She leaned on her elbows, set her chin on the backs of her laced fingers. "I hope your wife likes the ring."

"I'm sure she will."

"She's one lucky woman."

Gil had walked several blocks before realizing what Nadine had said.

CHAPTER 20

THE FLOOR WAS SO COLD.

She lay on her side, huddled tightly, so tightly that her arms and knees ached. She could hear the television upstairs and strained, hoping the announcer would mention the date.

Everything would be so much easier if she just gave up, drifted away. Died. But something inside her wasn't ready. Her eyes, swollen from months of beatings, throbbed.

In the beginning, when he got angry he slapped her. Not every day, just when she cried too much. So she'd hold her lips tight, but the whimpering would escape and he'd hear her. All the time he said he was doing what was best for her, and if she just trusted him . . . trusted *just* him . . . they could have a wonderful life together. Why was she too stupid to see that?

But why couldn't he see she could never trust anyone who hurt her? Tormented her? She feared not for her life as much as she feared for her loss of trust in anyone—ever again. What kind of person would she be if—when—she finally got to go home? She prayed that person would be worth everything she was going through to save herself.

The cement was so hard. Unyielding, holding fast the gate that was bolted to it. Not like the warm dirt at the other house. She ran her long toenails along the cracked surface. Then she got a mental image of how she must look, lying there scratching like a giant wounded animal. And she stopped.

The first time he tried making love to her, she screamed so violently that he'd smashed her face with the full force of his large fist. She shuddered, wondering what monstrous event had shaped him into this man who knew so little about love that he didn't know the pain he brought her would make her feel nothing but hatred for him. Then her shiver grew into uncontrollable spasms thinking about his mother.

When she finally gave in to him, offered herself in return for any bit of kindness he could show her, he became insulted. Shouted that he didn't want her pity and hit her with anything he could find. Rope, pieces of rock, a chain.

The last attack had broken off her front teeth. Now she used the pain. Shocks of agony reminded her he was breaking her body. It was simply skin and bones. But he could never get deep inside at the fire she desperately stoked each day with hope and prayers.

He'd taken her clothes with him after the first month, when the stink got to be too much. She'd begged him to wash them or let her do it, but he never brought them back. Nothing moved him—not the pleading, not the promises to stay with him if only he'd let her outside the cage. Nothing.

She finally stopped begging and got angry. Spitting on him every time he came close. He'd retaliated by hanging her from the ceiling for a few hours every day. Sometimes he'd pull up a chair, sit inside the bars and drink his beer, entertained. She managed to scratch at him, leaving a few scars across his cheek. Why couldn't anyone see them? Wasn't there one sane, decent person out there who would wonder? Ask?

People are all the same, she thought, answering her own question. They don't see what they don't want to see. It's just the way things are. Nothing personal. But still she wondered, When was the last time someone had really looked at her? Looked *for* her?

She rocked herself, singing softly. "Jesus loves me, this I know. For the Bible tells me so . . ."

He said she stank like the pig she was and dragged the hose in from outside, spraying her off several times a week. He'd thrown in a bucket for her to use but then let the filth collect.

"It doesn't matter. It's only for a little while. You're going to be all right." She squeezed her shoulders.

At least, when she first met him there had been the work. And the other women. Their stories and jokes made the tedious jobs fun. He had been nice to her then. They'd go out for hamburgers or pizza, bring back food for everyone. Maybe she shouldn't have been such a good worker. Maybe he was right and this was all her own fault.

"No! You didn't do anything wrong."

A door slammed upstairs and she sat up. Please, help me, please. I'm down here. She screamed the words in her head but didn't dare voice them.

When she heard the prayer, she knew it was Sanite. It had been a miracle she hadn't gotten involved in her son's love life. Truly a miracle. That woman had the power.

She pried up a sharp corner of her small prison floor and dug with her long, cracked nail.

K...E...L...L...Y...

When I get out of here and bring the police back, this will be my proof, she assured herself. This will be the proof that will hang all of them.

CHAPTER 21

MITCHELL LASALLE SAT in front of the computer screen, staring. According to the report, Kelly Denoux had been missing for almost four months. He rubbed his temples. "Shit." The word blew from his lips more like a sigh than a profanity. He'd seen this report once before, but was now reading it with more interest.

Kelly Lynn Denoux: twenty-three-year-old Caucasian female. Five feet, four inches, one hundred thirty-five pounds. Born: Pittsburgh, Pennsylvania, moved to New Orleans six months ago, lived alone. No car. No dog. No husband or children. No outstanding debts. He stopped.

Every red-blooded, able-bodied person over the age of sixteen had more than a few outstanding credit-card balances. It was the American way. He continued. Last employer: Domino's Pizza, back up north in her hometown. Nothing noted for any local work. He scrolled farther down on the report and found that, as he suspected, Ms. Denoux had been receiving federal aid since arriving in Louisiana. Reported missing on June 10 by. . . whom? There was no name.

LaSalle looked for a phone number in Pittsburgh: family residence, mother, brother—anything. But according to the screen, Kelly had been in and out of foster homes all her life. When she hit legal age, her record turned from court appearances for legal guardianship and visitation battles between what he supposed to be her father and mother to charges of shoplifting and vandalism. Petty stuff.

She probably came to New Orleans because of some guy, stayed with friends, hooked up with the wrong kind of people. It happened too frequently. So who had missed Kelly enough to report her missing? Who had cared so little to fill in some of the blanks? Anonymous reports were never given much credence. No time or manpower. If only . . .

He leaned back into his padded chair and covered his face with his large hands. Within the darkness of his thoughts he tried honing in on her fear. She had been held against her will in the Laveau house. That much was obvious to him. The outline in the floor indicated some kind of cage. But why? Had she somehow escaped and killed Auntie Laveau? Or was she also dead? And if so, why had her body been removed and not Auntie's?

He pushed his bulk out of the chair and moved toward his phone at the exact minute it rang.

"LaSalle," he answered.

"Detective, it's Gil Hunt."

"What can I do for you, Mr. Hunt?"

"I found out something about Kelly Denoux today. Do you remember? The name on the back of that mask I gave you when we were first here."

LaSalle's hand tightened on the receiver. He was not about to admit to Gil that it had taken three separate incidents for him finally to check out the girl's name. "Yes, I remember, Mr. Hunt. She's a missing person—"

"I knew it!" Gil caught his breath. "Did you know she worked for the murdered woman . . . that Auntie Laveau person?"

"What? How did you find out that information?"

Gil explained about the mask in Nadine's store and talking to the woman about Kelly Denoux.

"She's been missing for several months," LaSalle said. "Odd you should call just as I was going over the report again. I had her pegged as being a prisoner all this time, but now that you've shed new light on this . . . Listen, can we have dinner tomorrow? I'll take you someplace real local and we can compare notes."

"Sure, why not? What's going on with the woman in the hospital?"

"She's stable and we hope she'll regain consciousness within the next few days. Can I pick you up at your hotel around seven?"

"I'll see you then."

LaSalle broke the connection. His train of thought had been interrupted and he had to make some notes. He'd have to return to the house in Algiers with a team, early in the day when the light was good. He picked up the phone to round up some men for tomorrow.

"Over here!" LaSalle shouted to the photographer. "I want all the walls, the floor, every corner of the room."

Once again LaSalle stood in the middle of the basement in the small house. Nothing had been touched since his last visit. The guys upstairs were going over things again for prints, but this time Kelly Denoux's prints. They grumbled that they'd done it right the first time.

"And be careful of that!" he barked at the photographer,

pointing at the square indentation in the dirt floor. "Take a few of that and don't disturb anything."

"What do you think it is?" the young guy with the camera asked.

"Don't know yet." He had ideas, but didn't share them.

"Mitch!" one of the cops upstairs shouted down into the basement. "What about the yard?"

"Did you check it out last time?" LaSalle shouted back.

"There wasn't any reason to."

"Hold on; I'm coming." LaSalle heaved his weight up the steep stairs.

He was met at the top by an Algiers cop he had worked with before, a pleasant young guy, Detective Jacques Mirel.

"Now that we've connected the Denoux girl with all this, we're talking kidnapping along with murder. Guess we should look at everything more closely," LaSalle said.

"Appears so," Mirel said, holding the back door open for LaSalle.

"You were born here, right, Mirel?" LaSalle asked as they walked along the narrow dirt path leading to an over-grown backyard.

"We've been here as far back as my grandfather can remember. Why?"

"What did you know about the murder victim?"

Mirel kicked at a bushel basket piled with decayed leaves. "She was the witch lady. You know every neigh-borhood has one of them. All us kids were always daring each other to ring her bell or throw something at her window."

"But the woman who died in there wasn't that old."

"It all depends which side of forty you're looking at her from, I guess."

"And voodoo? You saw some of the stuff under the stairs

in that basement. Did you ever hear about her being involved with that kind of thing?"

Mirel laughed. "I think any woman claiming to be a Laveau feels obligated to give it a try. But hell, I don't believe in any of that stuff."

LaSalle pulled aside a large tree branch. "That's strange."

"What is?" Mirel asked.

LaSalle crouched down. "Look at this," he said, pointing to a row of bricks and boards. "This whole yard is a mess. There's no order anywhere—it's more like a dump. Then, all of a sudden, one row of boards neatly stacked, and next to it, a row of bricks piled precisely on top of each other."

Mirel strained to see what the detective was looking at. "This isn't good," he said.

"Why?"

"Those who practice voodoo believe that things should be placed side by side . . . next to a grave."

LaSalle frowned. "I saw a shovel over there, by the tree. Could you get it for me?"

Mirel hurried back. Handing the shovel to the detective, he said, "Objects placed to the left of the grave bring more luck."

"Thanks." LaSalle stood and gingerly poked the pointed blade into the ground to the right of the boards.

"Awww, geez."

"What? What is it?" Mirel asked anxiously.

"Look at this," LaSalle said, pointing to a bracelet wrapped around wrist bones that used to be covered with flesh.

CHAPTER 22

GIL DIDN'T KNOW what made him come back to Physicians Hospital. But after telling Detective LaSalle what he'd found out about Kelly Denoux and getting no reaction, Gil just knew he had to see the old woman again. Maybe she could help him get some sort of closure before he left town.

He casually strolled the route he'd traveled the first time with LaSalle. But when he walked into her room, all he found was an empty bed.

"Looking for someone?" a nurse's aide asked.

"Well, yes, there was an elderly woman here a few days ago, she was in a coma ..."

"Oh, you mean Jane."

"She didn't . . . die . . . did she?" he asked.

"No, they just moved her down to three-fourteen. They're doing that all the time around here. You a relative? Gosh, I hope so, because poor old Jane hasn't had one visitor. At least not on any of my shifts."

Gil patiently waited for the teenager to stop talking before he jumped in with his question. "She's awake then?"

"No. Sorry."

"Then how do you know her name is Jane?"

"Oh"—she looked embarrassed—"since no one seems to know who she is, we've started calling her Jane Doe. It makes her more of a person, know what I mean?"

"Sure." Gil turned to find room 314. "And thanks."

The new room was brighter than the old one. Gil couldn't believe that it had been so easy just to walk in. But then he wondered what he'd expected—a scene from some old movie? It wasn't as if Jane Doe were connected to a mob family. This was a frail old lady who apparently didn't matter to anyone.

Her color looked better than the first time he'd visited. The IV was gone and Gil pulled a chair across the tiled floor and sat down. "Why would someone want to hurt you?" he asked mostly to himself.

"Because I know too much," the woman answered.

Gil jumped up from his chair, sending it skidding across the floor.

"Who are you?" a heavyset nurse asked as she rushed into the room.

"Ahh, my name's Gil Hunt. She spoke to me!"

"I know, she started coming around about ten minutes ago; the doctor's on his way down. Are you a relative?" The old woman struggled to sit up. Scrutinizing Gil, she squinted to see him better.

"Now, lie back, Jane, you've been through quite an ordeal." The nurse eased her back into the bed.

"Who the hell is this Jane you all keep talking about? My name's Rene. Rene Conde. And you"—she pointed to Gil—"I remember you and your pretty wife."

"Claire," Gil said. "Her name is Claire."

"Yes. I saw her on television."

At that moment the doctor arrived. Dressed in green scrubs, he seemed in constant motion even as he examined the woman. He spoke loudly, treating his patient as if she were deaf. "Follow my finger with your eyes—don't move your head," he ordered as he slowly moved his slender index finger from side to side. "Good."

"I have something to tell this young man," she told the doctor, pointing to Gil.

"That will have to wait, Ms. ..."

"Conde," she said, matching his loudness, "Rene Conde."

"Well, Ms. Conde, you'll have lots of time to visit with your son after I'm done."

Before Gil could correct the doctor, he was instructing the nurse to escort Gil out of the room and into the visitor's lounge.

Half an hour and two cups of coffee later, Gil was told that he could visit Rene Conde, but only for ten to fifteen minutes, as she needed her rest.

"The coast is clear, you can come on in," Rene told Gil when she saw him hesitating in the doorway.

He walked to the side of her bed, his hands in his pants pockets. He wondered how he could feel so glad to see the woman alert and yet be apprehensive as to what she wanted to tell him.

"I hate doctors, don't you?" she asked, smiling. "Always wanting to test this and test that. It's all just a scam to get your money."

Gil nodded. "Seems like it sometimes. But at least they got you better."

"Don't be silly. All they did was give me a safe place to rest until I woke up."

"Safe?" Gil asked. "Why would you need a safe place?"

Rene patted the edge of her bed. "Come sit here so we can talk."

Gil hadn't noticed it the first time he'd met the old woman in the cemetery but there was something in her smile that reminded him of his own mother and the recognition drew him closer to her.

"I've been having the strangest dreams. All day and all night, ever since I've been here. Now the trouble I'm having is figuring out if they *were* dreams. I need you to help me."

"If I can, sure." Gil didn't know if the woman was aware of Auntie Laveau's murder. He was uncertain as to what he should tell her but quickly decided he would answer any questions she had as honestly as he could.

"Were you here in the hospital visiting me a few days ago?"

"Yes."

"And was there a big man, some sort of a policeman, with you?"

"Yes."

Rene bit her bottom lip. "I'm so very sorry about lying to you and that nice wife of yours. I hope you'll forgive me. I never did anything like that before."

"Like what?" he asked. "I still don't understand."

"Oh, I thought I was so smart. I thought I could cheat Auntie. And look what it got me."

Gil had to hold himself back from hugging the poor woman. She looked so frail and helpless. But he kept reminding himself that she had tried to cheat his wife and ended up putting them both in danger.

"Oh, she was a horrible person. And she deserved bad things to happen to her. Bad things. But not ending up the way she did."

"Then you know?"

"Oh, I know she was murdered. That's a fact, I do." Before Gil could ask one of the many questions flooding through his brain, the large nurse returned.

"We've just received a call from a Detective LaSalle. He asked that no one be allowed to see Ms. Conde until he's had the chance to question her."

Gil stood to leave. Rene grabbed his sleeve. "Please, Mr. Hunt. Will you come to my house for dinner? After I'm back on my feet? Please?"

Again she smiled and he knew he would be meeting Rene Conde again.

CHAPTER 23

"IS THE BODY KELLY DENOUX'S?' Gil asked.

"No," Lasalle said. "We don't know who it is, but it's too far gone to be Denoux."

Gil shuddered and looked down at his plate. They were at Delmonico's, one of Emeril Lagasse's restaurants. Emeril had recently become a celebrity chef on the Food Network.

"Is this conversation ruining your dinner?" LaSalle asked, looking amused.

The grin on the detective's face gave Gil the resolve to continue eating. "No, not at all." He speared another piece of trout and popped it into his mouth. "Continue."

"We did a thorough search of the yard and found three other bodies. Forensics will do their job and identify them, but I'm sure they'll all turn out to be missing persons."

"So have your guys been looking for Kelly all this time?"

He sensed LaSalle's discomfort as the man cleared his throat.

"You see, Mr. Hunt—"

"Gil, please."

LaSalle hesitated and Gil thought he was going to insist on last names to keep things businesslike.

"All right, Gil. The report on Kelly Denoux being a missing person was called in anonymously. We don't usually investigate cases that are not reported by family members or, at least, an identifiable friend in the cases where there is no family."

"So the report was just . . . ignored?"

"Not ignored," LaSalle said, "not completely, anyway. We kept a file copy which was entered into the computer system where I found it."

"And you still don't know who made the call?"

"Not a clue."

Briefly, LaSalle gave Gil the background on Denoux and how she was originally from up north.

"Could she have gone back there? Maybe she was homesick?"

"No," LaSalle said, "I don't think so, not after what I found in the basement."

"So she's not in the house, and not buried in the backyard. Do you think it was Auntie Laveau who kidnapped her in the first place?"

"Her or somebody working with her," LaSalle said. "The only thing we know for a fact is she was in that basement, probably kept in some kind of a cage."

"That poor girl."

Both men seemed to lose their appetites. They called the waiter over and ordered an Abita beer each.

"So, what are you going to do next?" Gil asked.

"Check out Kelly's apartment."

"How did you find out where she lived?"

"I started by checking out utilities under her name," LaSalle said. "There weren't any."

"Her landlord could be paying them."

"Right, but I did find phone bills."

"What about the other people who worked for Laveau?"

LaSalle shrugged. "We don't know who they are."

"Nadine—that woman who told me about Kelly—said that sometimes a man made deliveries, and sometimes another woman."

"Maybe we're looking for a man," LaSalle said. "Maybe he kidnapped Kelly for Auntie Laveau, and then they had a falling-out."

"There's something I don't understand, Detective."

"What's that?"

"Don't kidnappers usually demand a ransom?" Gil asked.

"Usually."

"But in this case there was nobody to demand it from."

"Obviously she was kidnapped for an entirely different reason."

"And when you find that out, you'll find her, right?"

"Could be."

When they finished their beer, LaSalle paid the bill and they walked outside. The evening was chilly and the men started walking toward LaSalle's car.

"What now?" Gil asked.

"I'm beat from rooting around in that yard all day. All I want to do now is go home. I'll get an early start in the morning and check out Kelly's apartment."

"What about the woman in the hospital?" Gil asked. "Do you think she's involved somehow?"

"I don't know yet," LaSalle said. "Just because she woke up from her coma and can talk doesn't mean she said anything that helped us."

Gil looked up at the detective. "I've been wondering . . . what *did* she say?"

"She doesn't know what happened to her or how she ended up in the hospital. The doctors told me something, though."

"What's that?"

"Her injuries were not consistent with those found when a person is attacked."

"So what do they think put her in a coma?" Gil asked.

"They have no idea."

CHAPTER 24

WHEN GIL RETURNED to his hotel that night, the first thing he did was call Claire. He told her what he'd discovered about Kelly Denoux, filled her in on his short talk with Rene Conde and told her about having dinner with LaSalle.

"You're not going to start annoying Detective LaSalle by trying to get involved in his investigation, are you?" she asked. "Promise me, Gil. Promise you'll leave all the police work up to the . . . police."

"I didn't ask to go to dinner with him, he invited me. To compare notes, he said. Obviously, he wants my help." Actually Gil had had little more to tell LaSalle beyond the fact that Kelly Denoux worked for Auntie Laveau, but at least he had come up with something the detective hadn't already known.

"Gil . . ."

"Don't worry, sweetie. I'm not going to get involved. I have that appraisal in Shreveport to do, remember?"

"When are you heading over there?"

"This weekend," he said. "I'll call when I get a hotel."

"You don't have to call me every night, you know," she told him.

"Yes, I know I don't have to, but I want to."

"I love you," she said.

"Well, you should, I'm a helluva guy."

She ignored his cavalier remark. "Stay out of trouble, please?"

"I love you, too," he said.

"I mean it, Gil; take care of yourself for me."

"That's what I'm good at."

"Oh, please . . ."

The phone woke Gil early the next morning. He had gotten to bed late because he'd gone out walking on Bourbon Street until one A.M. There was something about the pulse of that area after midnight that fascinated him. The street was closed to traffic every night and people simply strolled, sometimes stopping in a shop or a club, but mostly just interacting out on the sidewalks. He learned that Mardi Gras was not the only time women flashed their breasts on Bourbon Street.

He didn't go into the gentlemen's clubs, just walked up and down the street by himself, stopping for a frozen daiquiri at one of the corner bars. It wasn't necessary actually to go into the clubs to see what they were selling. Semi-nude women stood in the doorways, or swung in and out of windows, although you rarely saw more of the girl on the swing than her long legs.

When he finally returned to his hotel he was slightly miffed that none of the women on the street had deemed him worthy to flash. Maybe he just looked too old to be worth the effort.

Or maybe he just looked too married.

He answered the phone groggily, since it was earlier than he would have liked to start the day. He knew so even though his eyes couldn't yet focus enough to see the bedside clock.

"Hello?"

"Mr. Hunt?" a woman's voice asked. "Is this Mr. Gil Hunt?"

"Yes," he said, rubbing his face with one hand. "Who's this?"

"This is Rene Conde. From the hospital? You came to see me?"

"Of course, Miss Conde—"

"You just call me Rene."

"Rene . . . is something wrong?"

"I'm out of the hospital," she said.

"What? They discharged you already? I thought the doctor would have kept you longer—"

"I got no insurance," she said. "They don't keep you long if you got no insurance."

"I guess not." Insurance was something Gil had done without before marrying Claire. Now he only had it because he was covered under her policy at the TV station.

"I'm home," she said. "Remember you said you would come and see me when I got home?"

He didn't remember if he had agreed to that or not but he said he did.

"Will you come for coffee, this afternoon?"

"All right," Gil said. He reached for the hotel pad on the table next to the bed, at the same time finally noticing the time was 9:20 A.M. "What's your address?"

She gave him a number on St. Anne.

"Isn't that the street where Marie Laveau had a house?" he asked, remembering his research.

"Yes," Rene said, "They say her ghost still walks here every Saint John's Eve."

"When is that?"

"In June."

At least he didn't have to worry about running into her now.

"Can you come at noon? I have things to tell you."

"I'll be—" he said, but he was talking to a dead line.

CHAPTER 25

GIL DIDN'T KNOW how Detective LaSalle would feel about his going to talk with Rene Conde, so he decided not to ask him beforehand, and not to tell him afterwards.

Rene lived in an apartment off a courtyard on St. Anne Street. The wooden door he went through to get into the courtyard was hanging from one hinge. The yard itself was not well tended, weeds grew up from between slate tiles. He wondered if the stories of Marie Laveau's ghost walking here during Saint John's Eve had anything to do with the condition.

The main building had been divided into several apartments. He found number 7 and knocked on the door.

Rene appeared, stared at him through the screen, then said, "You came," much the way she had in the hospital.

He'd seen the woman on three separate occasions prior to today's meeting. The first time when she met with him and Claire, trying to sell them the masks, and then twice in the hospital. She'd looked different all three times, and now looked different again.

Her complexion certainly had a better color than it had

in the hospital. Also, her hair was snow-white and so clean it seemed to shimmer. He guessed her age at somewhere between sixty and eighty.

"I have coffee ready," she said, "and beignets."

"Sounds good," he said.

"We can't have them outside because it's a mess," she complained. "Was a time it was real pretty around here."

"I'm sure it was."

"Come inside."

She led him through the small apartment, which seemed to consist of three rooms: the parlor, bedroom and kitchen. He saw a small bathroom off the kitchen.

"Sit," she said. "How do you like your coffee?"

He took a seat at a metal table with a yellow Formica top. It reminded him of the one his mother had when he was young. He'd also noticed, when in the parlor, that her sofa and chair were mismatched.

"Just black," he said, "no sugar."

She puttered and fussed and he decided not to rush her, but to let her get to the purpose of this meeting in her own time. After all, he had the time to spare right now.

When she had the coffee and beignets on the table, she sat opposite him and smiled.

"Thank you for cornin'."

Her accent also sounded different today. The first time she'd sounded more Haitian or Jamaican than anything else, obviously trying to fake the accent. In the hospital, he'd detected almost no accent at all, but she hadn't really said much at the time. Now he was picking up a slight Cajun accent—or perhaps it was more of a cadence than anything else.

"It's my pleasure," he said. "I wanted to see how you

were doing. I don't think it was very fair of the hospital to cut you loose the way it did."

She waved a wrinkled hand. "I expected it. Them hospitals they don't care if they cure ya or make you sick, as long as they kin charge ya." She pronounced the word "charge" as "chahg." Definitely Cajun.

"Rene," he said, "what was it you wanted to tell me? I got the impression it was very important."

"You can help me, Mr. Hunt," she said, "ah know you can."

"Help you with what?"

"Fuhst, ah want you to know ah didn't have nothin' to do with killin' Auntie Laveau."

"I never thought you did."

"Well," she said, "the policeman, he seemed to think so."

"That's his job—to suspect everyone."

"Ah tol' him ah worked for Auntie, and that was all."

"But," Gil said, "you also tried to steal her masks and sell them."

Rene had the good manners to blush. "Ah tol' you ah never did nothin' lahk that befo-ah."

The Cajun accent was getting thicker, and he was beginning to think this was put on as well.

"Rene," he said, "you're going to have to start being straight with me if you want my help."

"Straight?"

"Just like the first time we met. Your accent is slipping."

She stared at him for a few moments, then said, "Damn," and bit into a beignet.

He started in on his, washing it down with the strong coffee, and waited.

"I got to tell you," she said, "I ain't no saint."

"I didn't think so."

"I been on the edge." She sounded almost proud. "On the dole, on the con . . ."

"You've had a colorful life."

"I have," she laughed, "that's for sure."

Having been "on the con" would explain her use of accents, but he wondered how good she could have been at it when even he could detect slippage.

"I never was very good at connin' people," she said, as if she had read his mind.

"Rene—if that's your real name."

"It ain't, but it'll do."

"I don't need your history. I don't even really need to get to know you better," he said. "But I do need to know why you wanted to see me. What is it you think I can help you with?"

Now she ignored her coffee and started to brush the powdered sugar from her hands. The sound was like sandpaper. "Do you believe in voodoo, Mr. Hunt?"

"As what?" he asked. "As a religion? As a cult?"

"Do you believe in curses? How about zombies, and spells?"

"Well, I usually try to keep an open mind about most things," he said, "but I haven't really seen any evidence of the things you're talking about."

"But you know who Marie Laveau was? You mentioned her on the phone."

"I've done some research."

"Well, I'm about to tell you a lot more than you could ever find out from any book."

Gil put his coffee mug down, pushed away the beignets, folded his hands on the table and said, "I'm listening, Rene."

CHAPTER 26

WHILE GILL WAS LISTENING to Rene Conde's stories, Detective LaSalle was taking a look around Kelly Denoux's apartment.

She lived in a building on Esplanade, just outside the French Quarter. He presented himself to the landlord, showed his ID and was admitted.

"Thank you," he said, ushering the man out. "I'll call if I need anything else."

"B-b-ut—" the man stammered, as LaSalle closed the door in his face.

He had spent most of the morning going back and forth with forensics and the Medical Examiner, trying to come up with some names to go with the bodies they had found in Auntie Laveau's backyard.

He'd had some uniforms canvas the neighborhood. After all, how can a person bury bodies in her backyard without being seen? But it turned out there was so much wild growth around the yard that it was virtually hidden from view, even by the closest neighbor.

"Folks say strange things went on in that house," Detective Mirel told him over the phone, "and they didn't want to get too close."

"Strange things like voodoo?"

"Some say."

"Come on, Mirel," LaSalle said, "isn't voodoo a way of life for these people? Why would they be afraid?"

"Being afraid of voodoo is a way of life for these people, LaSalle. It's what they call being smart."

"And you? What do you think?"

"I have a healthy respect for the people who believe," Mirel said.

"But you don't?"

"No," he said, "I don't—but most of the folks around here do."

"All right," LaSalle had said, "keep canvasing. Maybe you'll find one person out there who saw something and isn't afraid to say so."

"We'll see," the other man said and hung up.

With nothing significant from the M.E. or forensics, he decided it was time to take a look at Kelly's apartment. He got the address from the Missing Persons Report and headed over there.

Now that he was inside, he wondered how she paid for the place. The building was old and not very upscale, but it still could not have been cheap.

He walked through the apartment once—kitchen, dining room, living room and bedroom. The living and dining rooms were actually one large room. First glance yielded nothing of interest, so he began his search in earnest. In this respect, LaSalle was no ordinary cop. He had seen others—even partners of his—tear a place apart in a search, with little or no regard for the fact that someone would have to put it back together afterwards.

True, if this were the scene of a homicide he probably would not have been so careful, but since Kelly was missing and not presumed dead at this point, he had some consideration for the fact that she might be coming back.

He opened drawers, searched, and closed them when he was convinced there was nothing of importance inside. He lifted seat cushions from chairs and the sofa, and replaced them. He did not see the need to slit the cushions or dump out sugar bowls. In fact, he really didn't know what he was looking for. He was hoping that all he'd have to do was poke around, and maybe something would come looking for him.

He left her bedroom for last, figuring that a young woman would keep her most valued possessions in there. Perhaps, if he was lucky, there might even be a diary, which would certainly tell him something about the woman she worked for. Maybe even mention boyfriends.

He spent more than half of his time in the apartment searching the bedroom and in the end came up with only one thing of any interest.

CHAPTER 27

WHEN KELLY HEARD the basement door open she cringed, tried to make herself smaller in a corner of her cell. She never knew when Jean came down if he was going to make love to her or beat her, feed her or berate her. She had learned very quickly that he considered all of these things to be acts of love.

Sometimes she wished she were still a prisoner in Auntie Laveau's basement. The cell had been larger, and the floor warmer. Also, the old woman had fed her regularly, if only to keep her strength up so she could continue working.

Kelly remembered the day she had gone to that tearoom and seen the little index card on the bulletin board there, advertising for an "artist." Maybe she'd only had a few art classes, but what did she have to lose?

So she responded to the ad and met Auntie Laveau who, at the time, seemed a kind, soft-spoken old woman who was running a small business out of her home. Her kitchen and living room were alive with women casting, painting and polishing Mardi Gras souvenirs, the majority being masks. It seemed an ideal way to make some extra money until she could figure out what to do with her life. And the other women, usually five or six others at a time, were chatty and friendly, in spite of the sweatshop-like atmosphere. She'd made some good friends, which made her life in New Orleans that much better. But the very best part of her new job was the discovery that she was good at something. Really good. Auntie said she was the fastest and most artistic worker she'd ever had.

Kelly hadn't been there very long when Auntie took her aside, confided that with her speed and artistic flair, Auntie felt confident enough to go ahead and try to sell her masks on TV "We're such a good team—you and I," Auntie had whispered. "The artist and the businesswoman. We can make a lot of money, that we can." Finally, Kelly felt connected to someone, to someplace.

But everything fell apart when Kelly found out about Auntie Laveau's voodoo practices, and, later still, her innate cruelty. She'd been about to quit the job she loved when one day Auntie took her helper, Jean, aside. That evening, after all the other women had gone home, Kelly was trying to get her nerve up to confront Auntie. Before she could say a word, Jean attacked her, dragged her screaming toward the basement. She was thrown down the stairs, and when she came to was lying inside a large cage.

Up to that point, Kelly had hardly spoken to Jean. However, after she became a prisoner Jean used to come down to visit when Auntie Laveau wasn't around. Soon, he was professing his love and promising to help her escape. All she had to do was say she loved him. She resisted for the longest time, until being imprisoned became more unbearable than the thought of sex with him. Until finally one day she found the words to say what he wanted to hear and he got her out of the house, into his car, and to another house. For a few hours she dared to believe she was safe.

She had been wrong. Being "loved" by Jean was infinitely worse. For Auntie it had been about power, but for Jean it was about sex and "love"—and his love came in a variety of horrible acts.

She heard his footsteps on the stairs. At Auntie's house she used to try to tell from that sound what mood he was in. But she had to give up. At this new house his moods hadn't changed as abruptly as they had at the old one. It didn't matter what frame of mind he was in coming down the stairs. It could change between the top step and the floor.

The light from the kitchen streamed down behind him and she could see his shadow. He was almost at the bottom when a woman called from the top.

"Jean, come up here, you."

"Mama," he said plaintively, like a small boy.

"You goin' mind me, you!" she snapped.

"Yes, Mama."

Kelly heard Jean's footsteps start back up the stairs and sighed with relief. A brief reprieve.

If he really loved me, she thought, he'd kill me and put an end to this torture.

CHAPTER 28

JEAN LATOUR CAME into the kitchen to find his mother standing with her hands on her hefty hips. He closed the basement door quietly behind him and turned to face her.

"Yes, Mama?"

"You let dat girl get in your head, you," Mama Latour said. "When you goin' be done wit' her?"

"I don't know. I still love her."

The old lady shook her head and clucked her tongue at him impatiently. "You got to be a man," she scolded. "Sooner or later, you hear?"

"I hear, Mama."

"Now I tell you what I hear," Mama said to him. "Dat woman out da hospital."

"She not under your spell no more?" Jean asked, looking surprised.

"No, sumt'in' interfere wit' me spell. You gon' have to go to St. Anne and finish de job."

"But, Mama—"

"When she gone ain't nobody gon' know what

happened. Den you be safe, and dat my job as you mudda, ta make you safe, me, eh?"

"Yes, Mama."

"Den when you come back we talk about what you gon' do 'bout dat girl in the base-mint."

"I wish I didn't love her," Jean whined.

Malvina Latour regarded her son gravely, then put out her heavy arms so he could come to her, bend and lay his head on her massive bosom. He was her grown son, twenty-four years old, but he still felt like her little boy in her embrace. Of course, that also had something to do with the fact that she weighed close to three hundred pounds, and he weighed one hundred and thirty soaking wet.

"You do dis fo' you mama," she said, "and den you mama gon' help you, hear?"

"Yes, Mama."

"De cards say it's time for you ta do sumtin' wit' dat girl."

"Yes, Mama."

She released him from her arms and he stepped back, towering over her.

"Now go," she said. "I don't know how much time we got before she talk to dat policeman."

"She's afraid of you, Mama. I know she is."

"Maybe not so much no more," she said, wagging a finger at him. "Go now!"

Her tone galvanized him into action and he literally ran out to his car.

She went back into the living room, to her altar, and stood before the picture of Saint Michael. There was a spell for everything, but they didn't hold tight forever. How lucky she was to have Jean, to do what the spells couldn't. In turn, she protected him and tried to help him get the things he wanted—like that girl downstairs. But it had been going on too long now, and something had to be done.

First Rene Conde had to be silenced before she talked too much. Why, she lamented, had Jean agreed to help Rene steal from Auntie Laveau? It was all that horrible woman's fault for tempting her son.

Rene Conde had even been Mama's friend at one time. But then came the day when Rene overheard Auntie talking long distance, all the way up to Saint Louis, about those masks of hers . . . and got greedy. Ahh, money—such a wicked thing. It was always the money that caused such big troubles.

Mama sighed and lit a candle.

Big money, Rene had told Jean, would come to the two of them if they could just get to the television lady first and make that stupid Kelly girl work for them. And so they schemed. When Jean told Mama what they had done, how Rene had fooled Mrs. Hunt, all she could do was cast her spell and hope for much good luck.

But then Auntie had gone and gotten herself killed. Stupid, stupid woman that she was.

Mama had conjured to make the bad luck stay away from their house, to make anyone who could hurt her son leave them alone. But that Mr. Hunt, he was outside the circle, didn't fear what he should have and he came back. If he happened to stumble onto the wrong information, he would have to be dealt with, too, but Mama wanted to avoid that.

If only her spell had kept Rene Conde in what the doctor's called a "coma," this wouldn't be happening now. It was lucky that Jean had seen the Hunt man with the police detective at the hospital, or they might not even have known that he was in the city.

The detective would be no problem. He needed evidence to work with, and Mama was going to make sure there was none of that. Oh, she knew the police had found bodies in Auntie Laveau's yard. Everyone in Algiers knew, but all that meant was that they were going to blame Auntie for killing them.

But that man, Hunt . . . well, he was the kind of person who asked questions, and that kind was always dangerous. Getting rid of Rene Conde would scare him, make him run back home to his pretty wife.

And then she could concentrate on dealing with the troublesome girl in the basement.

On the ferry from Algiers to the Quarter, Jean Latour sat and gnawed at his thumbnail. His mama just better not hurt Kelly while he was away. He loved his mama, was loyal to her, and even afraid of her, but if she hurt his girlfriend, he didn't know what he would do.

He wanted the ferry to go faster. He had to get to St. Anne Street, deal with Rene Conde, and hurry back to Algiers as fast as he could.

God damn Auntie Laveau for dying like that. He hadn't hit her that hard. She'd just made him so mad. That's when all the bad luck started. There hadn't even been bad luck when he'd killed the first girl . . . what was her name? He searched his brain but couldn't come up with a name to go along with the face.

When Auntie found out about . . . the accident . . . she got real mad. And then, when he told her he loved Kelly and was taking her away, she threatened him. She was going to go to her altar and put a spell on him. He had to stop her, and hitting her with a hammer seemed the only way.

But he didn't have to worry about that; Mama was making everything right. She had never liked Auntie Laveau, even though she pretended she did. Auntie was always so uppity, claiming to be a descendant of Marie Laveau. Well, Mama was descended from Malvina Latour —and was even named after her. Malvina took the title of Queen from Laveau and Mama said that made Malvina greater than Marie.

He put his hand in his pocket to make sure he had his black cat bone. Mama's spells were going to fix everything— with a little help from him.

CHAPTER 29

"I'M TELLIN' you things I can't tell the police," Rene
Conde confided to Gil.

"And why is that, Rene?"

She looked at him as if he wasn't grasping what she was
saying to him. "For that reason—you're not the police. You
can't arrest me."

Gil frowned. He hoped she wasn't going to tell him that
she had killed Auntie Laveau.

"It was Jean," she said. "I'm sure of it."

"Who is Jean?"

"Jean Latour. He worked for Auntie."

"Doing what?" Gil asked.

"Everything. Heavy lifting, deliveries and, I think,
murder."

Gil still didn't understand. "And you don't want to tell
the police this?"

Rene leaned forward, looming over the table. "My life is
in danger, Mr. Hunt. Why can't you see that?"

"All the more reason to talk to Detective LaSalle."

"Let me tell you what I know for sure," she said, sitting back again, "then you can help me decide what to do."

Gil was trying not to upset the woman any further. Taking a deep breath, he asked, "But why me? Why are you telling me anything at all?"

"Because you were in my dreams, and . . . well, I don't have anyone else."

He now realized there was no logic in arguing with a dream and when he added in the fact that he felt sorry for her, Gil was ready to hear her out. "All right; what do you know?"

"Kelly Denoux was going to leave Auntie Laveau, like the others did . . . sooner or later."

"Others?"

"Girls who had come to work for her, over the years," Rene said.

"How many others?" he asked.

"Three or four. I'm not sure. Some of them worked for her before I got there. But I knew the two before Kelly, and they both disappeared."

"Left?" Gil asked. "Or disappeared?"

"Auntie said they left. But she told me she felt as though they had deserted her. She put a spell on them after they were gone."

"What kind of spell?"

"To make bad things happen to them."

"Like what?"

Rene shrugged. "Like dying."

"Rene"—Gil hoped he wasn't saying too much—"the police found four bodies in Auntie Laveau's backyard."

Rene's eyes widened. "It must have been Jean," she said. "He must have killed them."

"All right, calm down. You mentioned him before. Why do you think it was him?"

"Jean is . . . strange."

"In what way?" Gil wondered if he was doing this all wrong. LaSalle should have been the one questioning Rene. He'd know all the right things to ask and in a more efficient way.

"He said his mother was a mambo, a voodoo priestess descended from someone very powerful."

"Did he say who?"

"He didn't have to," she said. "His last name is Latour. I'm sure he was telling me without telling me that his mother is descended from Malvina Latour." She explained who Malvina was, and that she had succeeded Marie Laveau.

"So was Auntie Laveau also a mambo?"

"I think so," Rene said. "And I don't think there was any love lost between her and Malvina."

"So then why was Malvina's son working for her?"

"I have a theory about that," she said. "I think Malvina told her son to go work for Auntie. That way she would always know what was going on in that house. And I think Auntie liked the idea that she had gotten between Malvina and her son somehow."

"So if he was only there because his mother told him to be, why would he kill those girls?"

"I told you," Rene said, "he ain't right in the head. If he felt the same about those girls as he did about Kelly—"

"Whoa, wait a minute," Gil said. "How did he feel about Kelly?"

"He loved her."

"Are you sure?"

"I know a lovesick man when I see one," Rene said. "He

had it bad, and from the way he talked to me about some of the other girls, he loved them, too."

"I don't get it," Gil said. "If he loved them, why on earth would he kill them?"

"I think," Rene said, "because they didn't love him back."

"More theory?"

"Yes."

Gil understood now why she didn't go to the police. How much credence would they put in her theories? "So do you think Kelly is with Jean now?"

"Could be," she answered. "I believe that boy would have done anything to get her to love him."

"Did she ever tell you how she felt about him?"

"They didn't talk," Rene said. "She thought he was kind of odd, but as far as I know they never had a real conversation."

"And how well did you know Kelly?"

"We were . . . friends. Fact is I never had any children of my own, never got married. If I had a daughter . . ." She let it trail off.

"Rene, was Kelly missing while you were still working for Auntie?"

"Yes."

"And you called the police about her?"

"Yes," she said, "but they didn't let me finish. They took some information, but before I could tell them to check Auntie's house they hung up on me. Because I wouldn't give my name."

"So do you think she was still in Auntie's house, even after you reported her missing?"

"Something was fishy," Rene said. "Auntie wouldn't let

me go into the basement anymore. I think they had Kelly down there."

According to Detective LaSalle, that was the case. So if Rene had guessed right about that, Gil wondered, maybe she was right about the rest. "Rene, would Jean have killed Auntie to get Kelly away from her?" he asked.

"I think so," she said, "also . . ."

"Also . . . what?"

"I think he would have done it if his mother told him to."

"Okay," Gil said, "so, if he killed Auntie and took Kelly away with him, where would he have gone?"

"Probably to his mother's house."

"And where is that?" Gil asked, with growing excitement.

"I don't know," she said. "Maybe your detective friend can find out."

"And you won't talk to him?"

"No."

"Rene—"

"For one thing," she said sheepishly, "if he ran a check on me, let alone took my fingerprints, he'd find out my name isn't really Rene Conde."

That stopped Gil for a moment. "And under your real name are you . . . wanted somewhere?"

She looked away and said, "If I was I wouldn't tell you, would I?"

Okay, he thought, this is not about Rene, it's about who killed Auntie Laveau. And after that it's about who kidnapped Kelly Denoux, a poor young girl who may have actually been kidnapped . . . twice.

CHAPTER 30

JEAN LATOUR REACHED the house on Rue St. Anne. He stopped just in front of the courtyard and took the black cat bone out of his pocket.

Now invisible, if only in his head, he entered.

"What are you going to do?" Rene asked.

"I don't know," Gil said. "If I go to LaSalle with your theories, pose them as mine and not yours, he might think I'm nuts. I mean, how would I explain knowing any of this?"

"You just have to get him to look for Jean Latour."

"Maybe I can think up a story . . ."

"There's something else."

"Like what?" Gil asked warily.

"I don't want to be arrested, but I don't want to die, either."

"You think Jean will try to hurt you?"

"I'm sure he will."

"How do you know that?"

"Because his mother already tried."

"You'll have to explain—"

"That coma I was in," she said, leaning forward and lowering her voice, "it was a spell."

"Voodoo?"

Rene nodded.

"Then how did you come out of it?" Gil asked.

"I don't know that. But while I was in the hospital I did dream about you, then I heard your voice and woke up."

"So I woke you up from the co—the spell?"

"Maybe," she said. "How else do you explain it?"

"Well, you did hit your head—"

"When I fell. I'm sure I wasn't hit before then."

"So you think she'll try again?"

Rene nodded her head. "I'm sure of it, unless you find her and Jean first."

"Rene, then why don't you go to Detective LaSalle and let him protect you?"

"The police can't protect me from a mambo."

"Come on," he said, "do you really believe in all that?"

"I was under a spell," she said anxiously. "Listen to me, Gil, I'm not the gullible type. All my life I've been the one preying on other people's gullibility. But this . . . I can't explain this."

Gil could see Shreveport getting farther and farther away.

"Just try to convince your detective to look for Jean and Malvina Latour."

He stood up. "I'll try."

She stood up and walked him to the door.

Jean heard the voices from inside Rene Conde's apartment. He saw Rene and the man from the hospital. He tried to remember what his mama had said, tried to decide what was the right thing to do now that they were both here at the same time.

He gripped the black cat bone tightly in his hand, and decided to wait.

"Urn . . . one more thing," Rene said to Gil at the door. "What?"

"If you somehow had something to do with breaking the spell," she said slowly, "the mambo will have to get rid of you before she can hex me again."

CHAPTER 31

CLAIRE LOOKED INTO CAMERA 3. "It's a chilly day here in Saint Louis and as we've been hearing from our callers in the east, it appears that even though autumn has just begun, winter is coming upon us quickly. So be sure to get in on our deal of the day, a beautiful set of flannel sheets." She ran her hand over a pattern of ducks flying across a plaid background. "They come in this nature pattern as well as a solid blue and a whimsical teddy-bear print for the kid's room."

Harve Wilson, her director, spoke into a microphone hooked up to Claire's earpiece. "Be sure to mention the accessories."

Claire never missed a beat. "Matching comforters and pillow shams are also available. You can check the product number with our operators, who will be glad to help you find anything you need."

"Automated ordering," Harve said.

"Our phone lines are very busy now," Claire said. "So if you don't want to miss out on our best deal of the day, just call the number at the bottom of your screen. It's all so easy. Just follow the step-by-step instructions."

Claire could feel a headache coming on as she wrapped up her morning show. The last few years, her whole body seemed to respond to any change in the barometric pressure. Gil kidded her that she should work for the Weather Channel.

"Well, that's about it for me today." She sat down on the bed made up with the flannel sheets. "I'll see you tomorrow, when we'll have a special guest designer here to show you her beautiful sweaters that are designed and handmade in Italy. So until then, take care and stay happy." She sent a friendly wave into the camera and remained seated until Harve told her they had cut away to another segment.

"There's a tall handsome guy waiting to see you, Claire," one of the coordinators shouted as the hostess unclipped her mike. "He's in the break room."

The only thing on Claire's mind was going home and crawling back into her soft bed. This getting up at 4 A.M. was starting to wear thin. Maybe she could talk to Ben, the owner of the station, about a change. "Who is it?" she stopped to ask.

"Don't have a clue; never saw him before."

Claire tugged at her turtleneck. The damn thing seemed to be trying to choke her. She walked down the hall, hoping whoever had come to see her would say his piece and go away quickly.

When she stepped into the break room she was greeted by a friendly face and a smile that warmed her weary heart. "Yo, Mom!"

"Paul, honey, what a wonderful surprise." Claire wrapped her arms around the lean frame of her six-foot son.

"What are you doing here?" Disengaging her arms, she stood back quickly. "Is something wrong? You never come down here; are you okay?"

Paul laughed. "Didn't I tell you?" he asked an attractive young woman who remained seated at a nearby table. "Always happy to see me but always worried there's something wrong."

"My mom's like that too," the young woman said. Claire looked from her son to the young woman and then back to her son again. "Okay, now I'm confused. Do you two know each other?"

"I told you she was smart," Paul said.

"Stop it." Claire took a playful swipe at his arm. "Tell me what's going on."

"All right, all right." Paul held out his hands to the young woman. "Mom, I want you to meet Megan."

The girl stood up and came to stand by Paul's side. She flashed a smile that not only lit up her whole face but the entire room as well. "Mrs. Hunt, I'm so glad to meet you."

"Same here," Claire said, still a little confused.

"Mom," Paul said, pulling Megan closer to him. "This is the reason I moved back to Saint Louis."

Claire feigned a pout. "And all this time I thought it was because I missed you so much."

"That, too," he said, winking at Megan.

The three of them stood looking at each other for a few moments before Claire spoke. "Well, are you two hungry?"

"You know me, I can always eat," Paul said.

"Then I'll buy you guys some lunch and I can ask a lot of questions and get to know Megan and embarrass you," she said, looking up at Paul.

"Sounds great." Paul smiled. "Just as long as you don't

tell her all those endless stories about what an adorable baby I was or how smart I was in third grade or even how I always got the highest grades . . ."

"Your son certainly has one healthy ego," Megan said.

"You noticed that, did you?" Claire said. "I like her," she said to Paul.

The St. Louis Bread Company was a chain with dozens of locations in the area. Claire, Paul and Megan sat in a corner booth, eating from bread bowls filled with thick potato soup while they talked.

"So . . . tell me when you two met and why I wasn't informed," Claire said, sipping her Coke.

"In KC. Megan was on one of my tours, last summer."

"I took one look at him in that pin-striped suit and I was in love," she said, reaching over to touch his hand.

"So, you're into gangsters?" Claire asked.

"Not really," Megan said. "I was with some girlfriends; we were taking a road trip out to LA. We stopped in Kansas City to see all the fountains everyone's always talking about. Did you know that there are more fountains in Kansas City than in any city in Italy?"

"It's a beautiful place," Claire agreed.

"It was, once Megan got there," Paul joined in.

"Anyway," Megan continued, "we heard this commercial for a Gangster Tour on the radio, it sounded like fun. So we drove right over to the ticket office. We were about an hour early, but while we were waiting I spotted this gorgeous son of yours."

Paul dabbed at his newly grown beard with a paper napkin. "It was hard concentrating on what I was doing—I couldn't stop looking at her."

"Sounds like fate brought you together, that's for sure," Claire said.

"Especially when I heard she was from Saint Louis and was looking for her own place."

"I don't know how my folks are going to react to my new roommate, but I guess they'll adjust." She blushed ever so slightly.

Claire hid her surprise at the realization that the couple had been living together for a few weeks without telling her. But she liked Megan already. The girl's shiny dark hair swayed around her soft face each time she moved. She seemed so confident in her black T-shirt and jeans. Claire's gratitude to the girl for obviously making her son so happy overshadowed everything else.

They were still a little hungry when they had finished their soup and decided to indulge in one of the fancy pastries the restaurant was known for.

While they leisurely enjoyed one another's company and the hazelnut coffee, Paul suddenly asked, "How's Gil doing? Is he still in New Orleans?"

"Paul's told me so much about Gil, he calls him his pseudo-dad. I'm anxious to meet him," Megan said.

Claire smiled at her. "I hope you get the chance very soon. But I'm starting to get worried."

"See," Paul said to Megan, "I told you she worries."

"Stop kidding," Claire scolded. "He hasn't called for two nights."

"He's probably just all involved with his books. You know how he gets. And I always hear you telling him not to call you so much. Remember the time he went to Vegas without you and felt so guilty he called almost every hour . . ."

". . . for three days. That was different," Claire said,

giving in to the pangs of dread she had been feeling. "Something's wrong. I just know it."

CHAPTER 32

"CALL FOR YOU ON LINE FOUR," the voice interrupted LaSalle's train of thought. He'd come into the station
house early that morning for the sole purpose of organizing
notes for several cases he was working on. Angrily, he
jabbed the button on his phone.

"Detective LaSalle."

"Oh, I'm so glad I caught you, Detective. This is Claire
Hunt . . . you met with my husband, Gil and—"

"I remember you, Mrs. Hunt. How have you been?"

"Not so good. I'm concerned about Gil. I haven't heard
from him in a few days. Can you tell me the last time you
saw him?"

LaSalle thought a moment. "We had dinner two
nights ago."

"Did he mention any plans he had? Were you supposed
to meet with him again?" she asked, hoping something
would jog LaSalle's memory.

"He told me about an appraisal he was scheduled to do
in Shreveport. I got the impression he wanted to be there by
the weekend."

"That's what he told me, too. But this just isn't like him ... not to call me."

"Have you tried his hotel?" LaSalle asked.

Claire wondered if all the women LaSalle dealt with were as stupid as he assumed she was. "I called there last night. They said he doesn't answer his phone but he hasn't checked out."

"I don't know what else to tell you, Mrs. Hunt. Your husband seemed fine the last time I saw him. If I were you, I'd check out that appointment in Shreveport."

Claire tried to hold back her fears and said a controlled and quick good-bye to the detective.

The kitchen was the sunniest room in the condo and still Claire felt so chilled, she shook. "Gil, where are you?" she asked the air. Leafing through her phone book, she found Barbara and Huntley's number and called. Expecting to be greeted by their answering machine, she still hoped that maybe, by some stroke of luck, Huntley would be in town, in bed, just enjoying a day off. But when the recording came on, her heart sank as she left a message asking them to call her as soon as possible.

Next she called the Museum of the Dog. By this time she just needed to hear a friendly, reassuring voice on the other end of the line to allay the panic attack she could feel brewing in her stomach.

"Barbara's not in right now," the receptionist told her. "Can I have her call you?"

"Please. Tell her to call Claire Hunt as soon as she gets in. I'm at home." Then, without thinking, she added, "It's very important." As soon as the words had left her mouth, she wondered why she was getting so frantic.

"I'll do that, Mrs. Hunt. And you be sure to have a nice—"

Another call beeped in and Claire switched over without hesitation.

"Yes?"

"Claire, hi, it's Barbara. I got your message and—"

"You're at home?"

"I'm out riding. I called home for messages before I left the stable and couldn't stop thinking about how upset you sounded, so I decided to use my infernal cell phone. Are you okay?"

"No. I can't find Gil."

"I thought he was in New Orleans."

"He is . . . was . . . I don't know." Claire went on to fill Barbara in on what she had been doing for the past few hours. "So what I need now is to know if he made it to Shreveport. Do you know the name of Huntley's friend that Gil was going to meet? A number? Anything."

"Huntley's in Paris for two weeks."

"Oh, no . . ." Claire hated feeling so overwhelmed, helpless, and scared, but her emotions seemed to be on overdrive and the best she could do was try to steer straight.

"Relax," Barbara's soothing voice told her. "I'll go home right now and see if I can find something. Sit tight and I'll call you right back."

"Thank you so much." Claire slumped into a stiff dining room chair. "I hate to run you around like this . . ."

"Hey, no problem."

Waiting. Waiting. Claire had never been good at waiting. Her stomach grumbled and she tried eating something, but all she could manage was a cup of tea. She'd never loved anyone as much as she did Gil and now he was making her crazy. She had never felt this emotional when she was with Frank.

Her first marriage had been bumpy, but what did she know, she had been only seventeen, fresh out of high school. He was the boy next door, they'd met when she was thirteen. She thought he was rude, didn't like his friends. But, like mold, he grew on her.

Their first apartment had been so small, she smiled remembering how there had been only one closet. She could sit in the middle of the miniature kitchen and reach the refrigerator, stove or sink. But every time she got settled, Frank got itchy. And so they moved. And moved. It never had anything to do with his job; Frank just got bored.

By the time Paul was born, two years later, they had packed and unpacked six times. Claire wanted a home for more than a few months, especially now that they had a baby. Frank was still bored.

"If only he beat me or drank or gambled away all our money," she often told friends. But Frank didn't do any of those things. He never gave his wife one good reason to leave him. Her parents had come to love their moody son-in-law . . . at times she thought they loved him more than they did their own daughter. But now all the memories of that time in her life were painted in grays.

Because she'd met Gil. Gil, so full of joy and passion. They laughed at the same things, cried at the same movies. She used to believe that opposites attract but now knew how wonderful it was to be with someone she could understand and relate to. He often told her that they both had to go through years of unhappiness to become the people they were today. Mature people able to appreciate fully not only who they were but what they had found in the other person. She totally agreed.

Before she could let loose a flood of tears, the phone rang. She reached for the cordless by her hand. "Hello."

"Claire, it's Barbara."

"Oh, I was hoping it was you. So, what did you find?"

"It's that old good news/bad news thing, I'm afraid."

"Start with the good and then I'll see if I can handle the bad."

"Just when I walked into the door, Huntley called. It was as if he had ESP or something. And he gave me the number."

"You're a doll," Claire said, looking for a pen. "And tell Huntley thanks, too."

"Claire, I called down to Shreveport so you wouldn't have to."

"You really are a doll. So tell me . . ."

"The bad news . . ."

Claire braced herself. "Go ahead."

"Gil was supposed to call to set things up and they haven't heard a word from him. He's not there. I'm so sorry, Claire."

CHAPTER 33

SHIT, YOU DIDN'T have to be so abrupt with that poor woman, LaSalle scolded himself. After all, if it hadn't been for you asking him to come back down here, the poor guy would be at home, where he belongs. Sometimes you can be a real hard-ass, he told himself.

Swiveling around in his chair, he started to type. When he was finished he spell-checked the letter. Then he reread it to make sure the manager of the Bourbon Orleans Hotel would completely understand the official request.

This office is requesting you keep the room registered to guest Gil Hunt reserved under that name until further notice. It is imperative you notify Detective Mitchell LaSalle at the number above should anyone—repeat—anyone inquire about Mr. Hunt or attempt to gain access to his room. Please also advise all house-keeping personnel to stay out of the room.

Nothing is to be disturbed. This request will remain in effect until further notice from this office.

Should anyone in the hotel see Mr. Hunt or know anything about his whereabouts, they are asked to call this office immediately.

Satisfied with the letter, he faxed it over to the hotel. Okay, at least now he could continue his day guilt-free. Gil had seemed like a decent guy; he'd hate to think that he might be in trouble.

He gathered up the notes he'd been reviewing before Claire Hunt had called. LaSalle shook his head, Gil's probably over at the casino, just lost track of time. Maybe that wife of his is the hysterical type and he needed some time on his own. Just to get a little crazy, have some fun . . . New Orleans was certainly the place to do all those things.

"Awww, hell," he groaned. "Maybe I'd better stop by the hotel before I go home tonight. Just to make sure they got the fax."

He's coming! Oh, no, God help me! He's coming!

Kelly Denoux crawled to the far corner of her cage and curled up so tightly she thought her ribs would break. The voice in her head was screaming at a maddening pitch today. She must be close to going over the edge, she thought. He's beating me down . . . he's killing me.

The footsteps grew louder but there was something else. A dragging sound. He'd take a step, then pull, take a few more steps, then pull. She listened but didn't turn her head toward the light at the bottom of the stairs.

She tried concentrating on something inside her head. What day was it? Friday, maybe Saturday. At first she'd taken great pride in the fact that she always knew what day it was. Anything to keep her mind working—to make her feel human.

Then the second month had worn her down and the beatings had started taking more than bits of her skin, they'd taken chunks of her courage and determination.

Now, all those incalculable weeks later, she didn't even know if it was day or night. And she didn't care. She slept almost all the time, saving her strength to fight him off. Nursing her sanity in case she ever got out of here.

He banged into the cage and she was startled. Peeking under her arm, she saw him reach into his pocket. He came up with a fist of keys, all held together with a piece of wire. She also noticed a bundle at his feet, on the floor.

Jean unlocked the door and dragged the something on the floor into the cage. It moaned. Jean kicked at it and then quickly left the cage, never looking in her direction.

Thank you, God! She dared not even blink.

He snapped the lock on the cage shut, then started for the stairs. Adjusting his pants, he stopped, looking back at her briefly, then walked slowly up the stairs.

The light went out when he reached the top and snapped the switch from there.

Oh, God! she thought. Please help me. What has this maniac put in here with me? Oh, God, help me, she screamed without saying a word. But she knew—whether it was inside her head or outside—no one was listening anymore.

"I'm going with you, Mom," Paul said.

"No, honey. Maybe I'm overreacting . . ."

"Hello? This is your son here. We both know you're not the helpless-girlie type."

"But yesterday you said—"

"Hey, I was just yankin' your chain, Mom. Relax."

"That's the point, I can't. No one knows where Gil is. If I lose him I don't know what I'll do."

"You're not gonna lose him, they'd have to pry him away from you with a crowbar. Now haul out your credit card and get us two round-trip tickets to New Orleans because I'm going with you . . . and the move here took all my extra cash."

"But what about your job?" she asked.

"I haven't even been there a month. Besides, it's only part-time."

Claire was so grateful her son wanted to go with her; she hadn't looked forward to making the trip alone. But she couldn't ask him to drop everything now that he was building a new life for himself . . . even though she wanted

"What about Megan?"

"She's fine, Mom. And if she gets lonely she can have her sister come stay with her. Now stop making excuses for me. Hang up the phone and call the airlines."

"Yes, sir," she said.

"Oh, and Mom?"

"Yeah, honey?"

"I love you."

CHAPTER 34

"WHAT YOU GON' an' done, you?" Mama shouted at Jean. "I tell you get rid of Rene, not bring some strange man in my house." She swung her large hand and cuffed her trembling son on the side of his head.

He never knew when her anger would erupt and jumped with surprise. *"He's* the reason your spell didn't keep her quiet. *He's* the one been going to the police. And as long as he's here, he can't talk to no one."

She shook her head, lamenting the pitiful logic her son always seemed to fall victim to. Leaning in nearer to his face, she rested her hands on her knees, getting as close to him as she could. "Now listen, you. Wit both of dem down there now, we askin' dem police to come lookin', hear? We danglin' dem like bait. See now what I be tellin' you?" She waited for his brain to wake up.

He rocked his weight back and forth in the chair, all the time staring at his fingernails. She had told him when he was a kid in school that staring like that was supposed to bring good luck. It also helped him stop from gagging at her breath, which smelled of rot from that bad tooth in the back of her mouth.

"I had the cat bone. No one saw me, Mama. You know how that makes me invisible."

"Let's hope so." She straightened up and rubbed her back. "For you an' me, baby boy, let's hope so."

She walked into the kitchen and he looked up, glad for the respite from her anger but puzzled by her departure. He got up and followed her.

"I have a plan, Mama. I thought about this all the way back. It's a good plan, too."

She picked up a large wooden spoon and started stirring the gumbo she'd put on the stove earlier. "Tell it to me den, boy."

"When I helped Auntie . . . with those other girls . . . she . . ."

Mama stopped dead, turned and asked, "What odder girls?"

"The ones who were gonna leave her. They were bitches. No-good, stupid bitches who deserved to die. No one missed them."

"Auntie told you to do such a ting? Kill dem odder girls?"

"Well . . . sort of."

"An' after you do dis, what Auntie do?"

"Buried 'em, behind her house."

Mama had to sit down. "How long you been doin' such tings for Auntie, huh? You tell me now, Jean!"

His brain always got foggy when it came to numbers and days. But he managed to tell his mama enough of the right words to make her leave him standing there while she ran to her altar.

Again he followed her. "What you doin' now?"

"Gettin' me juju sticks."

"You casting a wanga? Who you wanna kill?"

"Dere's only one out dere who can hurt us, now. I take care of dem"—she pointed down toward the basement—"dey can wait. But her . . . Get me da rum, now."

Jean ran toward the cabinet in the kitchen.

Mama lit two candles, then shook her rattle gently while she said a silent prayer. When Jean returned, she grabbed the bottle from him. Carefully, she poured the alcohol into an empty glass which had been brought to the altar the night before—just in case she needed it. Filling it to the top, she then stuck one of the juju sticks into the glass. Jean stood behind her; she could feel his breath on her neck. "We wait now."

"For what?" her son asked.

"To see if de stick, it be thirsty."

The two of them watched as the dry stick absorbed some of the liquid. Slowly the level in the glass sank down.

"It worked." Mama seemed relieved. Then, closing her eyes, she slowly repeated the name, "Rene Conde . . . Rene Conde . . . Rene Conde," until it had been released into the air seven times. "Now quick, boy, go get me a lock."

"From where?" he whined.

"Don't matter to me none," she said. "Just be quick about it."

Frowning, he turned to do as she asked.

When he returned, she closed the lock over the end of the juju stick. "Dere now, it be done."

"What, Mama? What's gonna happen?" he asked.

"Rene be dead when the sun, it go down."

CHAPTER 35

"DETECTIVE LASALLE?"

"Yes?" LaSalle said into the phone.

"It's Officer Peltron, sir, the desk officer?"

"What is it, Officer Peltron?" LaSalle did not look up from his paperwork.

"Sir, I have an irate woman and her son here. They say they have to see you."

"What do they want?"

"They won't talk to anyone but you, and they won't leave. The lady says her name is Claire Hunt."

LaSalle looked up from his work and put his pen down. He suddenly felt like a little boy whose teacher had shown up at his home to speak to his parents. "All right, officer. I'll be right out."

He left his office and hurried to the front lobby, slowing down when he got there so it wouldn't appear he'd been rushing. He saw Claire standing in front of Officer Peltron's desk with a young man who stood about six feet tall and appeared to be in his early twenties. Her son?

"Mrs. Hunt?"

"I have had it!" Claire said, turning to him. "You ask my husband to come down here; he could have given you a hard time, but all he's ever done is cooperate. Then when I ask you for some information, some help, some simple courtesy, because I think something's happened to him, you treat me like . . . like some kind of . . . of inconvenience. Well, I'll tell you what inconvenience is, Detective. It's having to come down here and do your job for you!"

"Mom . . ." the young man said, putting a hand on her shoulder.

"You want me to call someone, Detective?" Peltron asked from behind the desk.

"No, it's fine," LaSalle said. "I'll handle it, officer."

"I'm not here to be handled, Detective—"

"Mom," the young man said calmly, "let the man talk."

"Mrs. Hunt . . . Mr. Hunt?"

"No," Paul said, "my name's Paul Duncan."

"Paul is my son," Claire said.

"Why don't you both come back to my desk, where we can talk?"

Claire took a deep cleansing breath and nodded.

"This way, please," LaSalle said, and led the way.

They followed him down a hall to a room with about half a dozen desks in it. Only one, besides LaSalle's, was being used. The walls of the room were painted institutional green.

"Please," he said, moving around behind his desk, "have a seat."

Paul skidded two chairs over in front of the desk and he and Claire sat.

"Mrs. Hunt, you're right, and I apologize. I was distracted when you called and I should have taken more time to talk—"

"Damn right you should apologize!" She realized she had the man on the defensive here, and was determined to make the most of it for as long as it lasted. "Thanks to you my husband is missing. He might even be . . . in terrible danger. Then, on top of everything else, I can't even get into his room at the hotel! The entire staff at that place looks at me and my son as though we've done something wrong . . . like we're criminals. I feel victimized here, Detective LaSalle." She said his name as though it tasted bad. Folding her arms tightly in front of herself she took a deep breath, fixing him with a glare while taking an instant to compose herself.

LaSalle stole a glance at Paul, who simply shrugged. He'd decided to let the detective try to handle his mother on his own.

"Mrs. Hunt—" LaSalle started, but he'd waited too long because by now Claire had gotten her second wind.

"After an hour of showing identification and pleading, the manager agreed to find us rooms at another hotel because his is all booked up. But only after telling us that he couldn't let us into my husband's room because of orders from the Almighty and Powerful Detective LaSalle. My own husband's room!"

"Mrs. Hunt," LaSalle tried again, but still no luck.

"We got in late last night, we were shuffled around and interrogated. We're angry, tired, and don't even want to be here! Do you think you could help us out, Detective? Just a little? Or is your schedule too busy?"

Finally. She was finished.

Mitchell LaSalle could be charming when he wanted to be. Seeing Claire Hunt so anxious and hearing her fear underneath the anger, he wanted to charm her into some semblance of calm.

"Mrs. Hunt," he said, "let me tell you why I gave orders that no one was to enter your husband's room."

Claire stared at the large man, waiting for him to offer some intelligent words. She crossed her legs tightly, held firmly on to the handle of her totebag. She clenched her teeth, making her jaw ache.

"Contrary to what you may think, Mrs. Hunt, I like your husband; he's a decent man. And for that reason I went over to the hotel last night and looked around. There were no signs of a struggle. Everything seemed to be in order. I don't think he was kidnapped."

"At least not from the hotel," Paul said. "It could have been from someplace else."

"Well, yes, there's always that possibility."

"Then do something!" Claire said, shaking uncontrollably.

LaSalle held up the papers he had been reviewing before Claire and Paul had interrupted him. "I am, Mrs. Hunt. I've been going over the notes I made after my dinner with Gil. I also have the lab reports from the murder scene, photos. I plan to start an official investigation today."

"What do you want us to do?" Paul asked.

"Nothing."

"Nothing?" Claire asked. "How can you expect us to just . . . wait. I'll go crazy if I don't do something."

LaSalle looked at Paul, afraid he would antagonize Claire even further. "I can't direct all my attention to the investigation if I'm worried about you two getting in trouble. Please, you ask me to do my job . . . stay out of this and let me. If something happened to Gil because of the questions he was asking about the Laveau woman, the same thing could happen to one of you if you start poking around."

Claire bit the inside of her cheek and continued listening.

Paul thought for a moment, then, without looking to his mother, said, "You're right, Detective. We'll give you as much room as you need."

"Can you at least tell the manager at Gil's hotel to let us into his room?" she asked. "I want to get his things."

"I'd rather you didn't remove anything just yet. I want a technician to go over the room first. If everything checks out, we'll send his things to you in Saint Louis."

"If that's the best you can do, I'll take it," Claire said as she started to stand up. "So, we're back where we started. You don't know where Gil is—I certainly don't. There are no clues and Paul and I can't do anything but wait . . . and worry."

LaSalle and Paul stood at the same time. "I guess you're right."

"Thanks, Detective," Paul said. "We'll be at the Hotel Saint Louis."

"You'll be going back home tomorrow, then? To Missouri?" LaSalle asked.

"Maybe," Claire said.

"I'll call when we find out something," LaSalle said, "I have your home phone on file."

"Thanks." Claire turned and headed for the door, with Paul trailing after her. "For nothing," she added under her breath.

CHAPTER 36

"YOU'RE GOOD, PAUL," Claire said as she picked at her salad. "When you make your eyes all big and sincere like that, the way you used to do when you wanted a Star Wars toy or some extra money."

"Give me a break, Mom; I was six years old then."

"Yeah, well, it took me a few years to catch on. But now you're this grown-up man and I still see you workin' it. I think Detective LaSalle really thought you were the polite kid just looking after his deranged mother."

Paul licked his fingers after putting his sausage po'boy back onto the plate. "I knew you understood what I was doing, Mom. We've always been connected like that, haven't we?"

They had gone back to the Bourbon Orleans Hotel and were having lunch in the restaurant off the lobby.

"Sure have." Claire buttered a roll and then put it down next to her salad. From the instant Paul was born she had felt linked to him in ways she could never explain to anyone. When he was small, all she had to do was think that it was time for him to come in and he would appear at the door. She remembered asking him once how he knew she wanted him. He told her he had heard her calling him in his head.

"And when you were giving Detective LaSalle all that stuff about 'If that's the best you can do,' and how we'll be going home tomorrow, I knew you didn't mean any of it. So once it was clear that he wasn't going to help us, all we had to do was get out of there and talk this thing through until we came up with a plan."

"You got that one right," she said.

They finished their lunch, watching the people around them, keeping their eyes directed toward the registration desk as well as the large front doors of the building.

Paul motioned toward his lunch. "They do have great food in this city. I'll have to watch myself."

"Don't worry, we'll be doing enough walking to work it off."

He looked at her with concern. "You haven't been eating very much. A salad is just a bunch of lettuce and air. You need real food, Mom. How about some dessert? You know how you love your chocolate."

"I'm not really hungry, hon."

Before Paul could think of anything that might cheer her up, a uniformed policeman entered the hotel with a plainclothesman in tow. One carried a large suitcase and the other was loaded down with a camera case and tripod. "Looks like our stakeout is over. And I didn't even get to finish my sandwich," he complained.

Claire grabbed her purse and motioned to the waiter for their check. "Do you see Detective LaSalle? Is he with them?"

Paul craned his neck. "No, it looks like just the two."

"Great; now you stay with them and call me with the number."

"I can't believe Gil never told you what his room number was," he said.

"He was always too busy telling me how much he missed me. But from now on, if I ever let him out of my sight again, I'll know exactly where he is," Claire said.

Paul took one last bite of his sandwich, then swiped his face with the napkin. Standing, he ran his hands down the front of his black jeans to brush off any stray crumbs. "See ya," he said and then started after the men, who were being ushered to the elevator by the manager. He was relieved to see his name tag read "Day Manager," and knew this was not the man who had been on duty when the two tried to check into Gil's room the night before.

Claire looked at the check and threw down enough money to cover the two meals plus a decent tip. Then she casually walked over to one of the high-back chairs in the lobby, settled in, and waited.

Ten minutes passed before she heard the announcement: "June Cleaver, paging June Cleaver."

Claire couldn't help but laugh at the inside joke. Paul's favorite TV show throughout his entire childhood had been "Leave it to Beaver." One summer he even had her hooked on reruns that they watched together every morning.

Walking to a house phone, Claire picked it up. "This is June Cleaver," she told the operator. "You have a call for me?"

"Hold a moment while I connect you."

"Mom," Paul whispered. "I'm in the hall on the fourth floor. They went into four-eighteen and the uniformed man is leaving."

"Good, that means there's only one. I'll be right up."

Claire hurried toward the bank of elevators. She watched the light above the doors signal someone was coming down. When she saw the cop step out of the elevator, she went up.

The manager stood in the open doorway, wondering if he should stay or return to work—close the door or leave it open and stand guard. Nothing like this had ever happened on his shift before. Maybe he should call his boss. No, Gus had left strict orders that he was not to be disturbed today. He was taking his girlfriend to the track and didn't want his wife to know he had taken the day off.

While he watched the technician, he was caught offguard by the sudden appearance of a young, pleasant-looking man.

"Look, Mom," Paul said, motioning to Claire, "the rooms here are awesome."

The manager held up his hands. "Sorry, sir, but I can't let you—"

"It'll only take minute." Paul towered over the man and gently pushed past him, all the while smiling.

Claire caught the manager's eye and started talking in a fast, clipped pace. "Don't they grow up fast? Why, it seems like just the other day he was in diapers and now he's getting married. He and his fiancée, they're planning a big wedding, right here in your hotel."

"Hey, kid, ya can't come in here," The plainclothed technician shouted to Paul.

"Honey, don't bother anything," Claire said, pushing her way into Gil's bedroom. Glancing back, she mentally noted how helpless the manager appeared and knew she could get what she wanted.

The cop standing in the middle of the large bedroom looked first to the manager and then to Paul. Claire knew the men would dismiss her as just . . . a woman . . . and she took advantage of her invisibility to study the room.

Both men tried talking to Paul, who went into his MTV summer-break persona. "Cindy will love this place! New Orleans rules!"

"Look, kid," the cop said, "I'm working here, this is off limits."

"Sure, sure, I just need to see the view." Paul stepped over to the window. Both men turned to follow him.

Claire took mental snapshots. But it was all she could do not to break down and cry when she caught sight of her husband's slippers on the floor. His scent seemed to linger in the air and she found herself blinking rapidly to keep the tears from streaming down her cheeks.

The policeman finally had enough of the situation and politely ordered them to leave. Relieved that the problem had been handled for him, the manager escorted Paul and Claire to the door.

"Sorry, but this is a crime scene and nothing can be disturbed." He walked with them to the elevator.

"Excellent." Paul smirked. "Totally excellent."

CHAPTER 37

FROM THE HEADACHE AND NAUSEA, Gil knew he had been drugged. The metallic taste in his mouth made him cringe as he tried figuring out where he was. Straining to move his arms, he realized after a few moments that they were tied down tight against his body. His head was in some sort of hood; from the smell of paint and dirt, he surmised he was wrapped in a drop cloth of some sort. When he stretched out, his shoes banged into the bars of his cage. He froze, afraid the noise might have alerted someone standing guard over him.

Instead of trying to get free, he listened. He lay stiff and breathed slowly, deeply, trying to avoid moving his body. After a few moments, however, he knew he wasn't alone.

"Are you all right?" a female voice asked.

A trick. He was afraid to trust anyone and remained silent.

He could feel hands tugging at his ropes. "Look, he'll be back soon, so let me know if you're okay or not."

Gil held his breath.

"You're locked in here with me. I've been kidnapped—

same as you."

He lifted his head slightly off the floor. In a low voice he cautiously asked, "Are you Kelly Denoux?"

Her fingers stopped working the knots. "How did you know that?"

"The police are looking for you."

"Oh my God," she said between sobs, "someone missed me."

Gil suddenly realized what he had said. "Kelly, you can't let on that you know what I told you. These people won't have any choice but to get rid of us—right away—if they think the police are coming."

Kelly leaned down and whispered in Gil's ear, "You're right. So, I'm sorry, but I better leave you tied up. Jean gets real mad. If he thinks I helped you, he'll never stop beatin' on me."

"Is Jean the one who kidnapped you?"

"Shhhhh. He's upstairs with Mama. He's the one got you, too, I heard them talkin'. This is Mama Latour's house an' she's got a way with voodoo. She's powerful. I bet she knows about you and the police already—even if Jean don't."

Gil tried to ignore his fear; his heart was beating like a triphammer. He had to think. There was always a solution to any problem, he just hadn't thought of it yet. If he concentrated, blocked out the terror, he'd come up with a way out . . . a way back to Claire.

Rene Conde didn't want to go out. She hadn't felt right for several days. It wasn't just because she had been in the hospital and the doctors had filled her up with all sorts of drugs while she lay there helpless. It was also because of the terror that brewed inside her, wouldn't give her one calm moment since Auntie Laveau was murdered. But there was nothing to eat in the house and she needed cigarettes.

Walking out into the bright sunlight, she was struck by how cold she felt. It had been warmer than usual for this time of year, and yet she needed to button her wool sweater all the way up to her neck. Must be the guilt, she thought, causing her blood to run colder. She had done so many bad things for such a long time. Maybe she was being made to pay for her sins by always feeling so uncomfortable inside her own skin.

The grocery store on the corner had a heavy rusted gate chained across the front door. She shook her head, mumbling to herself about the drugs and alcohol making people crazy. The store had been open just last week; now one more of her favorite places was gone forever.

She continued walking another two blocks until she reached a small market sandwiched between a souvenir shop and a bar. She hurried inside, glad for the shade. Her eyes hurt.

The place smelled of bananas and felt damp. She went down the narrow aisles, picking up the few things she couldn't live without: a loaf of bread, a small bag of coffee, marshmallow cookies, a wedge of cheese and some eggs. When she had laid all her items on the counter, she noticed the small TV set the clerk was watching and wondered about Gil and that TV wife of his. She hadn't heard from him since his visit. The least he could do was let her know if he had gone to the police with the information she gave him. Maybe there'd be a message from him when she got home.

"Is that all?" the tattooed clerk asked.

She pointed to the display behind him. "Two packs of Camels."

He rang up the sale and while she fished around in her pocket for some money, he put her things in a plastic bag.

"Have a nice day," he said, looking back at the TV.

Lifting her bag off the counter, she walked back out into the sun.

After maintaining a steady pace for a block, she could stand it no longer and dug the cigarettes out of her bag. Stopping to light one up, she inhaled deeply. Slowly blowing the smoke toward the street, she felt calmer, especially after rationalizing that as long as Gil Hunt was out there, Mama and Jean Latour would leave her alone.

"I hate to admit this," Claire said to her son, "But that was fun."

"My mother, living on the edge of the law." Paul kicked off his black tennis shoes and spread out on the bed in his hotel room.

Claire slouched down in the chair by the desk and propped her feet up on the bed. "I've been feeling so helpless. I just wanted to control the situation . . . any situation."

"Stick it to 'em, is what you want to do."

"You are *so* right. I have had it up to here"—she pointed to the ceiling—"with all of them telling me what I can and cannot do. I haven't done anything wrong—neither has Gil. I know there's crime everywhere. That the police have to be left alone to do their job, but hell, they're always asking for tips. Like on that show with John Walsh? But when we try to offer some help, we get patted on the head and told to go away."

Paul knew better than to try and interrupt his mother

when she took off like this. It was best just to lie back and wait until she ran out of steam.

"Of course there has to be some sort of system; we live in a civilized society and there has to be order. But this is Gil we're talking about. One person's been murdered, there could be another, and I don't intend to lose my husband without a fight. We just found each other." Her voice started to crack. "I will *not* lose him now. I need him too much." She covered her face with her hands. She'd always been embarrassed to let anyone see her cry, especially her son, for whom she was supposed to be strong.

Paul came around to where his mother sat, knelt down and hugged her. "I love him too, Mom, you know. He's the dad . . . I should have had."

"I didn't know you felt that way," she said, looking at him.

"After the divorce Dad not only shut down with you, he turned away from me, too. I've tried so hard with him and I never get anything back."

Claire felt that old guilt again. "I'm so sorry. But I planned and waited until you were a teenager. Your dad and I laid everything out for you, we made it clear nothing was ever your fault."

"You did everything right, Mom. I don't blame you for wanting to leave Dad, I could tell you weren't happy. Shit just happens. Dad's—just Dad."

One of those moments slid between them. No words could fill the space. She was so proud of the man her boy had become that all she could do was hug him.

They finally broke the mood at the same time. "Okay, so let's compare notes," she said. "Tell me what you saw in the hotel."

Paul got up and sat on the edge of the bed. "Dirty

clothes in a corner, a box of books on the desk. The bed was made, so I guess the maid had done that, or . . . Gil was sleeping with a stripper on Bourbon Street that last night."

"Very funny," Claire said. "Did you notice the little gift bag on the table by the window? It was white with red printing."

"Yeah, I did. I remember thinking that Gil had bought something for you. It just looked . . . girlie."

"I had the same thought. The only time Gil goes into boutiques like that is to buy something for me."

"And you know how he loves starting up conversations with waitresses and clerks."

"So maybe someone there will remember him, or at least we can get the day that he was there. I guess it's a place to start, since nothing else caught my eye."

"Sounds good, it's still early enough for all the stores to be open," Paul said.

Claire stood up. "I'll go clean myself up; you look in the phone book for the address of that store . . ."

"It was Accents, I'm sure of it."

"Okay, you call and I'll get ready."

"Oh, Mom," Paul said, reaching into his pocket, "maybe you'd like this, too."

She looked at the piece of paper he handed her. Recognizing Gil's handwriting, she asked, "What's this?"

"It was on the floor, near the window, Gil must have dropped it. Do you know who this Rene Conde is?"

Claire read the address and the time Gil and Rene had arranged to meet. There was no mention of the date. "And you just walked off with this?" she asked her son. "Right in front of the police?"

"Yep." He grinned.

"That's my boy." She grinned back.

CHAPTER 38

ROYAL STREET WAS CRAWLING with tourists.
Claire followed quickly behind Paul as he pushed his way
through the crowd. The afternoon was turning cool and she
would have enjoyed the walk if not for the purpose
behind it.

They found Accents without any problems and Claire
knew that Gil would never believe how the two of them had
maneuvered the streets so efficiently. He always liked to say
that Paul was directionally impaired but had come by it
honestly because he was Claire's son.

As they entered the store, she immediately knew why
Gil had been drawn inside. It was the kind of place she
would have spent hours in.

A woman approached them. "Hi, can I help you find
something?" She pushed aside the long hair that fell across
her forehead.

Paul stood looking at a poster on the wall, letting Claire
take the lead.

"I think my husband was here a few days ago. He might
have probably come in to buy something for me."

The woman looked as though she didn't have a clue what Claire expected from her.

Thinking it best that she begin again, Claire held out her hand. "Hi, I'm Claire Hunt. I live in Saint Louis and my husband was here, in New Orleans, on business this week. I think he may have come into your shop to get me a souvenir of some sort."

The clerk had looked puzzled until Claire mentioned Saint Louis and then she brightened up. "You must be the second wife! What's your birthstone?" she asked, testing Claire.

"Sapphire."

"And what does your husband do for a living?"

Claire would answer any question if it meant she'd end up with information about Gil. "He owns his own business, a bookstore."

"Right!"

"So you remember him?" Claire asked.

"Sure do, he was a real cutie. What happened? Did you misplace him?"

"Kind of . . . he's missing."

"Oh, my God, that's horrible." Her playfulness vanished and she looked sincerely upset. "The police haven't been here. I'd know, I'm the only one here most the time. They are trying to find him, aren't they?"

Claire rolled her eyes. "In their own good time. I just happened to see a gift bag from your store in his room, and thought maybe I could find something out on my own."

"Yeah, the cops have their own agenda. I have to tell you, Claire, I really admire you for what you're doing. It can't be easy." The woman smiled and for the first time Claire noticed how pretty she was. "By the way, my name's

Nadine, I'm the owner. Can I get you something? Coffee? A soft drink?"

"No, thanks . . ."

"You must be frantic," Nadine continued, "I know I would be. Hey, why don't you come in the back with me and I can look through my receipts, get you a date or time you can take to the police. I remember Gil used a credit card."

Claire appreciated the woman's eagerness to help but couldn't help wondering why she was being so nice. Hearing that she remembered Gil's name made her uneasy —or was it jealous?

She looked across the room. "That's my son, Paul." She wanted Nadine to know she had not come in alone and there would be someone waiting for her. Claire was also aware of how easily she and Nadine were communicating and decided not to change the mix by introducing Paul into their conversation. "I'm sure he can watch things out here for you while we talk."

"Sure." Nadine waved to Paul. "Hold down the fort, kid."

"I'll do my best," he answered.

It took about fifteen minutes for the two to talk through Gil's visit. Nadine finished by apologizing that she didn't know where Gil had gone after he left the store. Claire thanked the woman for all her kindness.

They went back out into the store.

"Good luck, Claire." Nadine hugged her. "That husband of yours is one of the good guys. I have your number at the hotel; I'll be sure to call if I remember anything else."

"Thanks so much. And your store is great, maybe another time I can come back and do some serious shopping. I like your sweater."

"And I like your man." Nadine smiled smugly.

Claire felt that pang of jealousy again and signaled to Paul that they would be leaving.

"Wait a minute! I can't believe I didn't remember to tell you about the mask!" Nadine practically screamed.

"What mask?"

"Gil saw this little ceramic mask I had and got all excited. Asked me questions about my supplier. About voodoo."

"Please . . ." Claire couldn't believe she might actually be running into a bit of luck. ". . . tell me your supplier was Auntie Laveau."

Nadine's eyes grew large. "How did you know? I have dozens of artists working for me. What are the chances?"

"And did the artists sign their work?" Claire asked.

"Always," Nadine said. "But this one really got Gil all charged up."

"Do you remember what the name was?"

"Sure. Kelly Denoux—she sometimes makes deliveries, too."

"When was the last time this Kelly came in here?" Claire asked. "I'd like to talk to her."

"Like I told Gil," Nadine said, "I haven't seen her for quite a while."

CHAPTER 39

WHERE WAS HE?

Rene Conde dialed Gil Hunt's room at the Bourbon Orleans again. She was getting anxious. Couldn't sit still. Couldn't concentrate.

After returning from the store, she'd made herself an omelette. Cleaned up the kitchen in her small apartment. Tried working through a few pages of that romance novel she'd started weeks ago. But her eyes wouldn't focus. She cleaned her reading glasses—even that didn't help much.

She went to the china cabinet in the living room and found a bottle of whiskey way in the back. Pouring herself a shot-glassful, she took it down in one gulp. Maybe that would warm her blood up. Get the heart pumping some good stuff through her body.

Walking back to the phone, she dialed Gil's hotel again and once more was told that he wasn't in his room. Would she like to leave a message? Of course she would.

And so for the fourth time in two hours she talked into the receiver at the sound of the voice-mail beep.

"Mr. Hunt, this is Rene Conde. Please call me about . . . what we discussed the other day. It's very important I hear from you very soon."

She flipped on the TV. Watched the news, looking for something . . . news about Auntie's murder, maybe the police had arrested someone. Maybe Gil was at the police station right this minute telling everything to that detective and Jean Latour was under arrest.

Maybe she was safe and didn't even know it.

Her skin seemed two sizes too small for her body and she scratched at her arms. If only she could breathe without the fear catching in her lungs, freezing up her heart.

She looked for her cigarettes and walked out into the courtyard to have a smoke. There was a nice big tree there and she could lean against it, not be seen too easily if someone was looking for her.

Her hand shook as she brought the tobacco to her mouth. The air was cooler now and she watched the sun slowly descending. Tomorrow would be better, she told herself. She was just getting all worked up over nothing. Neither Jean nor Mama had ever come to her home. They were cowards, hiding behind those superstitions of theirs, trying to make everyone afraid of them.

The last rays of the sun turned the clouds pink and gold.

Rene looked up and smiled as a cool breeze kissed her cheeks.

Tomorrow would be better, she reassured herself again.

Tossing the cigarette butt onto the ground, she stamped on it. Then, pulling her sweater tightly around her, she walked toward her screen door.

A pain shot through her shoulder and she doubled over from the shock of it.

Straightening up, she took a deep breath. When the stabbing had subsided, she started up the stairs.

The next pain caused her to fall backward. She was dead before her head hit the slate tiles.

CHAPTER 40

GIL SAT IN the cage and listened to Kelly Denoux answer all the questions his mind had been filled with for the past few days. He wished they were in a restaurant somewhere having this conversation, but that wasn't possible. At least he had convinced her to remove the hood that had been his blindfold. They had agreed that whenever they heard the basement door open she would quickly replace it. They didn't want Jean to know they had been talking.

While Kelly told her story, Gil studied her sadly. His heart went out to this dirty and beaten girl, who had been so forlorn until he told her people were actually looking for her. When a little hope touched her face, he could see the pretty girl who still lived beneath the torment.

"So I have to keep telling him that I love him," she finished. "I think that's the only reason I'm still alive."

"But he still beats you. Even when you tell him that?"

"Yes," she said, hanging her head, "he says when I deserve it, he has to, just to show me how much he loves me."

THE MASKS OF AUNTIE LAVEAU   169

"This is a sick man," Gil said. "You know that, don't you, Kelly?"

"Sure I do. But don't ever say that to his face," she pleaded. "It'll make him worse."

Gil wanted to explain to her that Jean was beyond reason and nothing he could say would change that, but instead he said, "Don't worry, I won't do anything to provoke him . . . for both our sakes."

Claire once again praised her son for having the presence of mind, and the nerve, to pick the piece of paper up from the floor in Gil's room. Then the two agreed that the next logical step in their hunt for Gil was to go to Rene Conde's house.

When they reached St. Anne Street they started checking the house numbers. The area was somewhat run down, and yet the homes still had a quaint look to them.

Paul—who had never been to the French Quarter before—commented on all the shutters.

"I know," Claire said. "The last time we were here, Gil said they should call this the Shuttered City."

Paul detected the catch in Claire's throat as she finished her sentence. He reached out and put his arm around her. "Don't worry, Mom, we're gonna find him. If we have to look behind every shutter in this city, we're gonna find him."

"We have to, Paul," she said, in a half-whisper, "we just have to."

"Look," he said suddenly, "there it is, across the street." They crossed over and found the address they wanted. According to the numbers, it appeared that Rene Conde's apartment would be in the back, off the courtyard. "Should we ring the front bell?" he wondered aloud.

"Let's try the gate first," Claire said. "I don't want to bother anyone else."

Paul shook his head. "You're too sweet, Mom. All you've been through and you still don't want to bother anyone."

"I know," she said. "I should be tearing the front door down with my bare hands!"

He put a comforting hand on her shoulder again. "Sorry, that's not your style."

She covered his hand with hers. "Have I said thank you for coming with me? I don't know if I could do this without you."

"There was never any question of you coming here alone," he assured her.

Together they opened the gate and stepped inside. They found themselves on a slate patio and had only taken a few steps when Claire's breath caught in her throat. It took Paul a second longer to see the woman lying at the foot of the stairs, a dark puddle of red spreading out from beneath her head.

"Oh my God," Claire said, putting her hands over her mouth, but unable to tear her eyes away.

"Mom—" Paul said thickly.

"That's her," Claire said. "Dear God, Paul, I think that's her!"

CHAPTER 41

GIL WAS IN the middle of telling Kelly what had been done so far to find her when they both heard the basement door open.

"Oh, God!" she whispered, frantically scrambling for the hood. "I have to get this back on you!"

"Take it easy," he whispered, ducking his head. "Just . . . that's it . . . slip it over . . ."

When the hood was on, he sat back and slumped his shoulders, hoping against hope that he looked the way the man had left him.

"Why you goin' down dare now?" a woman's voice called.

"I'm just gonna talk to Kelly, Mama."

"You got to decide what you want to do, you," she scolded him. "We don't be keepin' dat girl in me basement forever."

"I know," he whined.

"An' I don't know why you bring dat man into me house, either . . ."

"We been all through that, Mama. I'll take care of—"

"No, you don't take care of nuttin' with dat man till I tell you," Mama Latour said. "You just t'ink what you do 'bout dat girl."

"Yes, Mama."

"An' you come up soon, de gumbo, it be ready."

The door slammed and Gil heard footsteps on the stairs. He could feel the terror in the poor girl's body, even from his side of the cage. How could he help her? What could he do to help himself? What if Jean was coming for him, and not her?

Jean was mumbling to himself as he approached the cage. "Don' know why she treat me like I'm a kid," he grumbled. "I know what I'm doin'."

Gil heard Jean's hands grab the cage door and now he couldn't feel Kelly's terror because he was only aware of his own.

The steel door opened and Jean said, "Hey, mister? You awake?"

Should he answer? He decided to try a grunt and see what happened.

He felt Jean's hands on him, prodding him, but he didn't react.

"Guess you still got some of that drug in ya," he said. "Come here, girl."

"Jean, no—"

"Come on, now," he said, coaxing her. "Your Jean don' want you to think he's been forgettin' you."

"Jean-"

"Come on, damn it!"

Gil felt the cage move when Jean jerked Kelly outside the bars. He should shout, he thought, say something . . . do something . . . but what?

"Jean got to show you he loves you, Kelly."

"Jean . . . I love you, too."

"You been talking to that man?"

"No, Jean," she said. "He—he ain't said a word since you put him in there, honest."

"You not lyin' to me, are ya?"

"I wouldn't lie to you, Jean," Kelly said. "I love you."

Gil bit his lip as he heard the anguish in the girl's tone. He wanted to tear at the bonds that held him fast, but he was afraid to—and that fear made him ashamed.

Suddenly, he heard the sound of flesh on flesh—a smack, and a grunt of pain.

"Jean!"

"That's just a little of what you'll get if you talk to the man when he wakes up," Jean said. He hit her again and Gil flinched. What should he do if Jean decided to rape her? Could he just sit there and listen?

"You don't talk to the man, you hear?"

"I hear, I hear," Kelly whimpered. "Don't hit me again."

"Jean loves you, you know?"

"I know."

"And you love Jean?"

"I do, I do," she said, like an anxious bride, "I do, Jean."

"You get back in that cage, now," he said. "You filthy and you stink."

"I'm sorry, Jean," Gil heard her say as she crawled back into the cage.

"I come back later and hose you off," he said, "so you be nice and clean for your Jean. Then I show you how much I love you."

"Okay," she murmured, "okay."

Gil felt Jean's hand prod him again, then the man

grunted, closed the cage and went back up the stairs to have his dinner.

Kelly cried but Gil didn't have the nerve to speak to her. The shame he felt made his eyes burn and he was glad his face was hidden beneath the hood. He'd just sat there and listened to her get beaten. He hadn't done a thing.

CHAPTER 42

DETECTIVE LASALLE CAME out of the courtyard and walked over to where Claire and Paul were leaning against his unmarked car. He'd instructed them to wait there for him and not move. For once, Claire was doing what she was told. She had her arms folded across her stomach and was wondering how long it would be before she'd actually be sick.

"Is she dead?" Paul asked.

"Oh, she's dead, all right."

Claire grabbed Paul's hand and squeezed it. "Murdered?" Paul asked.

"The M.E. says it looks like she had a massive heart attack, fell backward and hit her head on the slate."

"Was she . . . dead before she hit the ground?" Paul asked. He was feeling as sick as his mother, but he was still interested in the maudlin details. Maybe it was a holdover from his college days, where he had majored and got his degree in criminal justice.

"Who knows? There's a lot of blood, which doesn't

usually happen if the vic is already dead, but she did crack her head like an egg—"

"Please!" Claire said, covering her mouth.

"It's not pretty, is it, Mrs. Hunt?" LaSalle asked. "If you had stayed out of this whole thing like I asked you to, you wouldn't have to see this."

Now Claire realized that he'd been trying to make her sick and she became angry instead. "And when would you have found her if we hadn't, Detective?" she demanded. "When would you have gotten around to it?"

"Look," LaSalle said, becoming angry himself, "I'm all out of excuses and apologies, lady—"

"Hey!" Paul said belligerently, "don't talk to her like that."

LaSalle glared at Paul. He was bigger and heavier than the younger man, but Claire was proud that Paul did not back off, even though she could see him swallow his fear.

"Okay," LaSalle finally said, "I'm sorry, both of you. Look, you found her and I appreciate it, but—"

"How can you be sure she wasn't murdered?" Claire asked. "Maybe whoever took Gil did this."

"We won't be sure of anything until the M.E. does his autopsy."

"I want to know the outcome," Claire insisted.

LaSalle rubbed his big hand over his face and gave Paul an exasperated look. Paul refused to give the man any kind of look that might make it seem he sympathized with him. It was he and his mother against the detective, and he wouldn't have it any other way. This man was going to find out what a formidable team they were.

"She has a right—" Paul started, but LaSalle gave in before he could finish.

"All right, all right," he said. "Go back to your hotel. I'll call you there when I have the results."

"Tonight?" Claire asked.

"I doubt it," LaSalle said. "I'm sure the M.E.'s got a couple of clients ahead of this one. Probably tomorrow morning. If you've gone home by then, I'll call you—"

Claire pushed away from the car, her queasiness forgotten, and stood right in front of LaSalle. "Get this through your head, Detective. I'm not leaving New Orleans without my husband. Without him, I've got no reason to go home. Do you understand?"

In the face of Claire's passionate devotion to her husband and her marriage, LaSalle had no defense.

"I understand, ma'am," he said. "Go and get yourselves some dinner, then go back to your hotel. I'll give you a call in the morning."

"If you don't, I'll be back in your office," she said.

"Oh, I believe you, Mrs. Hunt," the detective said. "I believe you." He looked at Paul. "Take your mother away from here before the M.E.'s boys take the body out."

That suggestion was one Paul was willing to take. "Come on, Mom," he said, gently taking her arm, "he's right. Let's go."

They crossed the street together and Claire muttered, "Go have something to eat, he says. Who can eat?"

"Well," Paul said guiltily, "I am getting hungry."

Her son's cast-iron stomach never ceased to amaze her.

When LaSalle reentered the courtyard, the M.E. approached him.

"Can I have her now?"

"Sure, Doc," the detective said, "she's all yours."

"I suppose you want a rush on this one?"

"Quick as you can," LaSalle said. "I've got someone anxiously waiting for the results."

"I'll do what I can." The M.E. turned and waved to his men to bag the body.

LaSalle watched them, wondering if he would ever meet a woman who would be as passionate about him as Claire was about her husband.

Gil Hunt was one lucky man—at least, he would be if he managed to come out of this alive.

CHAPTER 43

MAMA LATOUR GLARED across the kitchen table at her son. She loved him dearly but he was a trial most of the time. He sat shoving gumbo into his mouth as if he didn't have a care in the world.

"When you finished your gumbo you best take back dat car you borrowed to bring dat man here."

"I will."

"You sure dat friend of yours not gon' say nuttin'?" she demanded.

"He don't even know why I wanted the car, Mama," Jean said. "Don't matter if he says nuthin'."

"Still," she said, "you take dat car back tonight, you."

"I said I will!"

"Don't sass me, boy!" She took a swipe at him.

He ducked his head and said, "Sorry, Mama."

"And I want you go 'round Rene Conde's apartment an' see what you can find out."

"You put a spell on her," Jean said. "She's dead."

"You check anyway. Make sure she dead, you hear?"

"Yes, Mama."

She got up and carried her bowl to the sink.

"Mama?"

"What, boy?"

"You ain't gonna do nuthin' to Kelly while I gone, are you?"

Mama turned and leaned against the sink. She folded her massive arms across her equally massive bosom. "What I gon' do to dat girl, you t'ink?"

"I don't know," Jean said, looking up from his dinner. His lips were smeared with the food. "You still pretty mad cause I brung her here."

"I mad," Mama said. "But I ain't gon' do nuttin' 'cause you love dat girl—but if she don't love you back soon, you gon' have to do some'ting, hear?"

"I hear."

"Maybe you wan' me make a love spell for her, after all?"

"No. Can't force no girl to love me. She got to love me all her own."

Mama shook her head. She loved him dearly, but what girl was gonna love her Jean all on her own?

"Finish you gumbo and git," she said.

"Yes, Mama."

Downstairs, Gil finally worked up the courage to speak to Kelly.

"Kelly?"

She didn't answer. Maybe she'd fallen asleep?

He called her name again, a bit louder.

"Shhh," she said urgently. "You want them to hear us?"

"Are you okay?" he asked, lowering his voice.

'Tm fine. He didn't hit me so hard this time."

"Oh," he said. "It sounded pretty bad to me."

"It's been worse."

"Can you . . . take the hood off?"

The next moment went on long enough for him to think she might not want to help him. But then she slid the fabric off and dropped it on the floor between them. He blinked his eyes, while they adjusted to the gloom. Whatever light came into the basement from some small windows was fading, but he could make out her face. There had been so many bruises to begin with, he couldn't tell if there were any new ones.

"I'm sorry," he said.

"For what?"

"For not trying to help you."

She stared at him as if he were crazy.

"What could you do? You're all tied up."

"I don't know . . . I could have yelled."

"Then he would have dragged you out of here and beat you, too."

"Kelly, we have to try and get out of here."

"We can't."

"But, if you untied me—"

"I can't do that!" she snapped, still keeping her voice low. "If he found out, he'd kill me."

"Not if we escaped."

She hesitated, then said with her head down, "I've tried. I can't get away."

"Maybe you couldn't," Gil said, "but together we can."

She hesitated again, then lifted her head and looked at him. "How?"

CHAPTER 44

WHEN LASALLE RETURNED to his desk there was a pink message slip informing him that Detective Mirel from Algiers had called, and wanted him to call back.

"I checked up on that name you gave me," Mirel told LaSalle after they'd gotten past the usual greetings. "Jean Latour?"

Latour's name had been on a greeting card LaSalle had found in Kelly Denoux's room. It had been the only thing of interest, seemingly received from a boyfriend, or a would-be boyfriend.

"What'd you get?"

"Folks who lived around Auntie Laveau's house said Latour worked for her. They said the girls she employed came and went, but this Latour fella was with her a long time."

Because Laveau had kept no records of her workers, LaSalle had no names and addresses; therefore had not been able to question anyone who worked for her. Except for Rene Conde—and he wouldn't be finding out anything else from her, ever again. So he'd asked Mirel to try to come up with something on Jean Latour.

"Did you get an address?" he asked hopefully.

"Boy, that'd come in handy, huh?" Mirel said. "But no, not yet. I'll keep looking. Just wanted to check in."

"Okay, thanks."

He hung up and took the greeting card out of his desk. The handwriting was a childish scrawl, the card something a fourth grader would buy for a secret crush—only LaSalle didn't think Jean Latour was a fourth grader.

This case was dragging on, and driving him crazy. First Auntie Laveau had been killed, then Kelly Denoux came up missing, then Gil, and now Rene Conde was dead. Add to that the bodies they'd found in Auntie's backyard, and he had one hell of a mess.

So far the computers had not been able to match any missing persons to the bones forensics had found. The program was still being run, trying to match descriptions to bone breaks or old injuries found on the bodies.

He looked at his "in" box but found no report from the tech he'd sent to Gil's room. He didn't hold out much hope that the man would find anything. He knew he might get in trouble for allotting even the one man and equipment to a hotel room that was not technically a crime scene, but he felt he owed that much to the Hunts. If he got called on it he'd have to talk his way out of it.

But then . . . he'd done that before.

CHAPTER 45

CLAIRE AND PAUL COMPROMISED. He was hungry, she was tired and wanted to sit down and have a drink. Neither of them felt like looking for someplace new, so they decided to eat at Gil's hotel, since theirs was small and did not have a dining room.

Paul had a full meal while Claire just ordered a glass of wine.

"Now I've seen everything," she said, staring across the table at her son.

"What?" He looked up, chewing his shrimp.

"Even seeing a dead body can't kill your appetite," she said. "I'm more impressed than when I saw you eating a pizza while you watched *The Fly*."

"Seeing her dead made me glad we're alive. Feeling alive made me hungry."

She sighed. "I guess I can't blame you for that."

Paul continued to eat but noticed that his mother just stared toward the lobby while sipping her wine. When her glass was empty, he signaled the waiter for another Merlot for her and a beer for him.

"Is that good?" Claire asked, looking at the label.

"I like it, but Gil would know if it's quality stuff. He really knows his . . ." Immediately he felt bad. "Sorry, Mom."

"For what?" she asked. "We're not going to stop talking about him. After all, he's not dead . . . right?"

"Right." Paul sat back and wiped the crumbs from his beard with the red linen napkin. "I get it. Now I see why you wanted to eat here."

"Because it's convenient. Our hotel is right—"

"You're thinking we might see Gil. That he might just . . . appear. Walk through that door, never knowing that everyone's looking for him."

Claire stared down at the table. "Wouldn't it be wonderful? Of course I'd be furious with him"—she looked up at Paul with a sad smile on her face—"but you know how he gets wrapped up in those books of his."

"Yeah, sometimes he's like one of those absentminded professors."

"And after I got done screaming at him how worried we all were, I'd hug him so tight. I swear to God—after this is all over I will never let him get involved in any kind of mystery. I'm never going through this again."

"I don't blame you," Paul said. "And if he ever wants to play detective, I'll hold him down while you tie him up." Claire laughed but she knew that Gil's curiosity was one of the things she loved most about him. And even though that maddening curiosity of his had gotten them into all these messes—this one was her doing. She was the one who had talked to Auntie Laveau on the phone to begin with. She was the one who agreed to come to New Orleans to see those stupid masks, not knowing they were just cheap souvenirs. It was her fault Gil was missing, and that made it so much worse. She had to deal with not only the fear now but the guilt.

"Mom?"

She became aware that Paul had called her name several times. "Hmm? What?" She reached out and squeezed his hand. "I'm sorry."

"It's okay," he said. "I was just saying I wanted to go to my room and call Megan."

"Oh, sure, of course. Go on."

"I want you to come back to the hotel with me. I can't leave you here alone."

"That's sweet, Paul, but I'm a big girl—"

"Mom," he said, cutting her off, "I don't want to have to go looking for you, too. I couldn't take it if both of you were missing."

She smiled weakly at him and set her glass down.

"All right, let's go."

The only escape plan Gil could come up with meant that Kelly had to untie him. Then they'd wait for a chance to overpower Jean.

His explanation was interrupted when the basement door opened and they heard footsteps on the stairs. The light went on and Jean appeared at the cage door just as Kelly had gotten the hood back over Gil's head.

"You awake, mister?" Jean asked, once again poking Gil. Gil felt he had to answer this time. How much longer could he expect Jean to believe he was still unconscious?

"I'm awake."

Jean opened the door and handed in a bowl of gumbo and a spoon to Kelly.

"What about him?" Kelly asked, cradling the bowl in her dirty hands.

"He don't get any," Jean said, locking the door. "You got to keep your strength up. He ain't got no need to keep his."

Jean turned off the light and left the basement without any further explanation.

Kelly pulled the hood off Gil, who caught the scent of the food. It made his mouth water and his stomach growl.

"Smells good," he said. "He's right, you better eat. You'll need your strength if we're going to get out of here."

"D-do you want some?" she asked.

He did. The smell of the warm gumbo made him realize how ravenous he was, but he said no. "You've been down here a lot longer than I have. You need it. Go ahead and eat."

"We'll share," she said and brought a spoonful of the thick soup to his mouth.

He thought it was the best thing he'd ever tasted. As she ate her portion he asked, "So, are you with me, Kelly?"

"We'd be taking a big chance. If it didn't work, he'd probably kill us."

"He intends to kill me anyway," Gil said. "And maybe you, too, once he realizes you don't love him."

She gave him two more spoonfuls and then slurped down what remained at the bottom of the bowl. As she licked the spoon, Gil noticed a few drops had spilled down her chin and onto the front of her tattered shirt.

"I have to think," she said. "I—I need time to think about it."

"Not too much," Gil said. "I don't think we have all that much time left."

Instead of returning his friend's car right away, Jean took it with him to check out Rene Conde's street. Once he reached the Quarter it didn't take him long to learn of her death just by asking some of her neighbors if they knew where she was. Although the courtyard was sealed off with police tape, he could see the dark stain on the slate by craning his neck. Obviously, she had fallen down the stairs when she was struck by Mama's hex.

So now they were safe. Rene was dead, and that man Gil Hunt was in the basement, safe and sound, with Kelly. There was no one left who could hurt them.

Mama would be so happy.

CHAPTER 46

CLAIRE SPENT AN UNHAPPY, fretful night in her room, all the while thinking about Paul and how glad she was that he had someone. In light of the fact that she could end up losing Gil, she was very grateful to Megan for coming into Paul's life.

At midnight her phone rang and she leaped on it at the first ring, hoping it was Detective LaSalle with some news. "It's just me," Paul said. "I wanted to check on you."

"I'm fine, Paul."

"Are you really, Mom?"

"No, damn it. I'm scared to death."

"Have you tried to get some sleep?"

"No."

"Well, I'm beat. But if you want something or need to talk . . . just wake me up. Okay?"

"Don't worry about me so much, honey."

"I have to," he said. "You're the only mother I've got and I'd kinda like to keep you around for a while."

She felt tears welling up in her eyes and asked, "How's Megan?"

"Fine."

"I bet she misses you."

"Yes."

"And I also bet that you miss her."

"I know what you're doing, Mom," he said.

"What do you mean?"

"Changing the subject. Sure, I miss Megan, but I know where she is and I'll be seeing her soon. I also miss Gil. So, tell me, what should we do tomorrow? What's the plan?"

"I wish I knew," she said, rubbing her forehead. "I guess we're finally going to have to do what Detective LaSalle said and just wait for him to call."

"All right," he said, "but I'm going to take you someplace nice for breakfast."

"We'll see . . ."

"I'm not six years old anymore, Mom. 'We'll see' doesn't cut it anymore."

She knew she'd better give in. "Meet me in the lobby at ten."

"I'll come to your room and walk down with you," he said firmly.

"Yes, sir."

"Night, Mom. I love you."

"Love you, too."

After hanging up the receiver, Claire thought about how she used to kid her son by telling him that she always wanted a best friend and could never find one—so she had to make one herself. Now she knew how truly lucky she was to have such a good friend in her son.

LaSalle was in his office early the next morning, checking

his "in" box for the M.E.'s report. When he didn't find it, he picked up the phone.

"I was waiting for your call. I knew if I held on to this report, I'd be hearing from you."

"Why'd you want to talk to me?" LaSalle asked.

"Because this is an odd one, Detective."

"In what way?"

"Well, I've examined the dead woman's internal organs. While she obviously abused her body with cigarettes, alcohol and fatty foods, it was no worse than most people her age."

"Meaning what, Doc?"

"Meaning I can't find any good reason for this woman to be dead."

"No heart trouble?"

"She had a very healthy heart, from what I can see."

"Well, she did have a fall recently. What about some sort of head injury? A blood clot?"

"I checked everything," the doctor said. "Detective, as far as I'm concerned, this woman shouldn't be dead . . . except . . ."

"Except what?"

"Well, except for the look on her face."

"Doc, you've got me here. What do you mean?"

"You might think I'm crazy, but she looks like she was . . . well, scared to death."

"Scared? By what?"

"Either something she saw, or something she . . . felt."

Considering the talk about Auntie Laveau, LaSalle asked the doctor, "Do you believe in voodoo?"

"Well, now that depends on what you mean by believe—"

"Doc, could someone be frightened to death if they think they've been . . . cursed?"

"The mind is capable of convincing the body of practically anything. I've read about people making themselves sick and others recuperating from illnesses doctors thought were terminal. But by 'cursed,' are you saying that because someone chants some words, miles away from another person, they can cause harm? Maybe even death?"

"Well . . . stranger things have happened," LaSalle said.

"That's true," the M.E. agreed. "It makes about as much sense as anything else. But don't quote me on this or expect to see any hint of this in my report."

"Okay, Doc," LaSalle said, "send it over."

"On the way."

LaSalle hung up and was about to call Claire Hunt when the phone rang again.

"LaSalle."

"This is the operator downstairs, Detective," a woman's voice said. "I've got a lady on the phone who wants to talk to whoever is in charge of the death of somebody named Rene Conde. Supposed to have died yesterday on St. Anne—"

"That's all right, operator," LaSalle said, "Put her through."

CHAPTER 47

RAYMELLE ROBICHEAUX HAD NEVER LIKED Rene Conde very much. For one thing, the white lady was not a very good neighbor, had hardly ever spoken to Raymelle or any of the other folks in the area. Still, nobody deserved to die that way.

"What way was that, Miss Robicheaux?"

"It's Mrs. Robicheaux, and I'm talkin' about the way Rene died."

"You mean a heart attack?" LaSalle asked cautiously.

"Well, if you want to think she died of a heart attack, that's yore bizness, Mr. Detective, but there was a fella here yesterday askin' about her. If she died of a heart attack, why was he so interested? Folk die that way all the time."

"What fella, Mrs. Robicheaux?" LaSalle asked. "What was his name?"

"He didn't say his name, but he shore was in'erested in Rene. Wanted to know where she was, and din't look the least bit surprised when ah tol' him she was dead."

"Can you describe him for me?"

"Tall black fella, not bad-lookin', but I don't think he was all there, if ya know what ah mean."

Could it have been Jean Latour? LaSalle wondered. "What did he want to know exactly, ma'am?"

"Where Rene was, what she was doin'. Knocked on my door and a few others, askin' if anybody seen her. You ax me he knew she was dead all along, he was jest checkin'."

"On what?"

"On whether or not the spell worked."

"What spell?"

"Ah heard there weren't no mark on her body, and believe me, that woman was too healthy to have a heart attack. She used ta go up and down them stairs to her place real fast, and all the time luggin' heavy stuff—like groceries."

Of course, the healthiest person in the world could suddenly have a heart attack, LaSalle reasoned, but this, combined with what the M.E. had said . . .

"Mrs. Robicheaux, this is very important," he said slowly. "Is there anything else you can tell me about this fella asking the questions?"

"Only that he talked to a few of the others in the neighborhood. You kin talk to them if you want, but they gonna tell you what I tol' you."

"Maybe somebody noticed something you missed."

"Don't think so."

"Why not?"

"Ain't nobody in this area spends as much time at their window as me."

He waited, but when nothing else was forthcoming he asked, "Are you saying you saw something from your window?"

"Ain't that what a window is for?" she asked. "To see

things? Don't make a person bad if'n she wants to look out her window—"

"Mrs. Robicheaux? Please, could you just tell me what you saw?"

"Well . . . I saw it," she said. "He got into it and drove away. Pretty as you please."

"His car?" LaSalle asked, trying to remain patient with the woman. "Are you saying you saw his car?"

"Ain't that what I said?" she demanded.

"Yes, ma'am, you did. What kind of car was it?"

"Don't know nothin' 'bout cars," she said, " 'cept maybe the color, and this one was gray."

"And is that all you can tell me?"

"That's it," she said. "Don't know nothin' else. Didn't get his name, and I don't know nothin' about cars. But I thought I should call someone and tell them 'bout this suspicious fella. Din't feel right, know what I'm sayin'?"

"Yes, I do. And thank you for calling, Mrs. Robicheaux. We'll check out—"

"That's it, then?" She sounded disappointed.

"Unless you've thought of something else?"

"Nothin' . . . lessen you want the license plate number."

CHAPTER 48

WHEN LASALLE ACTUALLY did call at nine-thirty that morning, Claire was surprised. After all, he could have just blown her off, didn't have to keep his promise. For a moment she almost felt bad for tearing into him the night before.

Almost.

"I hope I didn't wake you, Mrs. Hunt," he said.

"No," she assured him, "I'm just waiting for my son, we're going to have some breakfast. Did you . . . find out anything?"

"Nothing very positive, I'm afraid," he said.

"Was Rene Conde . . . I mean, did she . . . was she murdered?"

"The Medical Examiner isn't quite . . . finished yet," LaSalle said. "He's . . . going to do some more tests."

She sensed he was lying, or stretching the truth. "He doesn't know how she died, does he?"

There was a pause, and then LaSalle said, "Hasn't got a clue. He says from the way her internal organs look, she shouldn't be dead."

"So what killed her?" she asked, and then, half-kidding, added, "voodoo?"

He didn't answer.

"Oh, come on, Detective, you don't believe—"

"I didn't say I believe in voodoo, Mrs. Hunt, but a lot of people around here do. This *is* New Orleans."

"Yes, but it's also the twenty-first century."

"I'd like to give you a name and see if you've ever heard it before; maybe Gil mentioned it one time when he called you?"

"Go ahead."

"Jean Latour."

She repeated it, then said, "From the way you pronounce it, I assume it's a man?"

"It is. Have you ever heard it before?"

"No, never," she said. "Is that who you think kidnapped Gil?"

"It's just a name I've come across," he said. "In fact, the only man's name. He might be a boyfriend, or a suitor, of Kelly Denoux's."

"Well, then, you have to find him."

"Exactly right, Mrs. Hunt," he said, "I do have to find him."

She was aware of how kind he was being and felt a slight twinge of guilt. "I'm sorry," she said, "of course you know that. Do you have . . . anything else to go on?"

"One or two things," he said. "I'll be checking them out today."

"Can you tell me?"

"I really can't; sorry, Mrs. Hunt. Not at this time."

"Well," she said, "you know where I'll be."

"Yes, I do," he said, "I'll keep you . . . informed."

"I appreciate this, Detective. It's very decent of you. Gil said you seemed like a good guy. I guess he was right."

"I like your husband, Mrs. Hunt," he said. "Don't worry, I'll find him for you."

"I like him too, Detective. And I hope you will."

Claire and Paul left the hotel and leisurely walked until they found a restaurant for breakfast. There was a red building on a corner. All the shutters were open to the mild breeze. The warm air felt soothing on her face.

"All right," Paul said, when they were seated. "Tell me what he said."

Over coffee and juice, while they waited for their food, she related the conversation she'd had with LaSalle to him.

"He didn't tell you very much, did he?"

"No, he didn't," Claire said, "but I think he told me more than he had to."

"You're giving him the benefit of the doubt today," Paul said. "Why?"

"I was kind of rough on him yesterday."

Paul's jaw dropped. "Well, I'm sure he understands you being a little upset. After all, your husband is missing, and we find a dead body. Gee, Mom, I think you have a right to be a little . . . impolite."

She nodded. "I know."

The waiter placed their omelets in front of them and refilled their coffee cups.

"So, what are we going to do now?" Paul asked. "We can't just sit around the hotel all day, and I'm not really interested in sightseeing. We need to do something constructive."

"After we finish our breakfast, we'll talk everything out," she suggested. "We'll work through all of it logically."

"Like they do in the books and movies?"

"Like Gil would do," she said.

CHAPTER 49

"I JUST THOUGHT OF SOMETHING," Paul said.

"What is it?"

They had finished breakfast and decided to walk down Bourbon Street until inspiration struck.

"You said this all started with a woman called Auntie Laveau, right?"

"It certainly did," Claire said, taking her sunglasses out of her purse.

"Well, I was reading some of the brochures in the hotel lobby," Paul said, "and there's a Marie Laveau Museum. They say it has an altar or a shrine to her."

"Where is it?"

"I don't know," Paul said, "but those brochures should be in the lobby of any hotel. There, let's cross over."

They walked across Bourbon and Claire waited outside while Paul went into a large hotel. When he came out he was brandishing a dark red pamphlet.

"This is it," he said. "It's the New Orleans Historic Voodoo Museum. Come on, we can walk."

"What do you think we're going to find there?" Claire asked, trying to keep pace with her long-legged son.

"I don't know," Paul said, "but it's something to do." Claire could not argue with that. It was better to be moving than to sit and wait.

The museum was disappointing. Even though the inside was draped with black gauzy fabric, and the bulk of the exhibits was devoted to voodoo, it reminded Claire of the gift shops she and Gil had visited during their first trip. There were voodoo dolls, candles in various colors, charms, pendants, beads, vials of oils and books of spells. There was even a tarot card reader in the back room.

After wandering through the gift shop proper, Claire found herself standing in front of a display of Mardi Gras masks, getting angry at herself all over again for ever getting involved with the cheap things.

On the other side of the store, Paul found a couple of slim volumes about Marie Laveau and decided to buy them.

He came up alongside Claire. Seeing her staring at the masks, he asked, "You're not thinking about buying one of those, are you?"

"No," she said bitterly. "I just want to smash them."

"Come on." He gently turned her toward the cash register. "I want to get these books."

She opened her purse and took out her wallet.

"I have money, Mom," Paul said.

"I know. I just don't want you spending any of it while you're here . . . because of me." She shoved a twenty-dollar bill at him.

He'd learned, long ago, not to argue with her when it came to money. "Thanks."

A petite girl with purple hair came up behind them and then walked around to the cash register. "How many?" she asked, smiling up at Paul.

"Two."

"You have to go behind that curtain." She pointed and Claire could see the girl's black nail polish matched her lipstick.

Paul looked confused. "You can't ring up these books for me here?"

The girl noticed the books for the first time. "Oh, sorry, dude, I thought you guys were here for a reading."

Before Claire could say anything, Paul asked, "How much is it?"

"Twenty."

"For one or two?"

"Twenty dollars per person," she said.

He handed her the bill Claire had just given him, then turned to his mother. "Come on . . . you know you want to." He smiled.

Claire wasn't surprised her son had known what she was thinking.

Leaving the books on the counter, Paul told the girl he'd be back for them when they were finished.

The man sat reading a worn romance novel. When he saw Claire and Paul peeking around the curtain, he quickly put the book down. "Come on in, I don't bite."

Paul laughed and held out his hand, "Hi, I'm—"

"No names, please," the man said, "just birth dates and where you currently reside."

Claire seated herself in a rattan chair that looked as if it belonged on a patio instead of in the small back room.

After shaking the man's hand, Paul sat down in a hard wooden chair next to the reader.

"It's okay if you know my name, though." The man smiled a benign smile, like someone who should be selling shoes rather than reading cards in a voodoo shop in New Orleans. "I'm Von, and I'll do my best to answer the questions you've come here with."

Claire wondered if the man began each session the same way. His words sounded rehearsed but she sensed his sincerity and had learned long ago her intuition seldom failed her. "Who first?" he asked.

Paul looked at Claire. "Oh, just one of us is getting a reading. Is it okay if I stay and listen, though?"

"Well, I don't normally . . ."

Claire shifted in her chair. "Please, I'd really like my son to stay."

Von studied Claire's face for a moment. "Okay."

"Thanks," Paul said and leaned back, trying to get comfortable while he watched.

The man reached under the table and brought up a purple velvet pouch. Untying the strings at the top, he reached in and withdrew a worn deck of tarot cards. Handing them to Claire, he said, "I need you to shuffle these for me and then divide them into three piles." While she did that, he neatly folded the pouch and laid it on the windowsill next to him.

Claire folded her hands in her lap when she was done.

"Now can I please have your birthday—month, day and year and the city in which you now live."

"September twenty-first, 1958. I live in Saint Louis, Missouri."

Von took the cards from the pile to his right and spread them out in a cross formation. "Royalty. I see kings and queens, lots of them. And a man who is your soul mate. You haven't known him long, but you were destined to meet, nothing could have stopped it."

Claire nodded.

Von asked Claire to shuffle the cards again and this time he laid all the cards out in a circle. After studying them for a moment, he said, "You're not here on a vacation, there's something wrong. Not business but personal, I see law officials around you. And water. You're surrounded by water."

Claire leaned closer. "Well, we are on the Mississippi River here, and in Saint Louis, too." She looked up and was met by the pale blue eyes of the man as she caught him staring at her.

"You're not as strong as you'd want everyone to think you are," he said softly. "All you want to do sometimes is to just . . . relax."

"The cards tell you that?" she asked.

"No. I can sense it."

"What else do the cards say?"

"One more time." He gathered the cards and pushed them toward her. "Shuffle once more and then cut the cards toward me."

After she was done, she waited.

Von spread the cards out again. "Water, and houses. Are you going on a cruise?"

"No," Claire said.

Paul couldn't sit still any longer. "Can you tell when our 'business' here will be done?" he asked. "And if we'll have success?"

"No." Von looked annoyed at the interruption. "But I can see it's been difficult for your mother."

"It's been difficult for a lot of people," Claire said.

The man read the cards for about ten more minutes

before glancing at his watch. "Well, I guess that's about it. Thank you for coming, and I wish you much success in the future, although it's clear that you'll always be lucky where your career is concerned."

Claire got up out of the chair and started to walk toward the door when Von stood up and grabbed both her hands. He hunched down a little, until his eyes were level with hers. "Remember, always pick the middle. The middle is always the right way to go."

"I will," she said, wondering what the hell he was talking about.

"Nice meeting you," he said to Paul. "Watch out for that royal family," he said, "you know how they can be."

"Yeah," Paul said. "Off with your head!"

CHAPTER 50

GIL WAS SHOCKED when he woke up—shocked that he had even been able to fall asleep. The hood was still on, so he had no idea what time it was, or whether night or day.

"Kelly?" he whispered, wondering if she was awake.

"Yes?"

Without being asked, she slid the hood off his head. Whatever light filtered in from the small basement windows caused him to squint for a few moments. He blinked until his vision cleared and then looked across the cage at her. If they both sat with their legs extended they'd be able to touch each other's feet. Gil could feel his legs cramping and he tried moving them.

"It's all right," she said, "you can stretch out. I know how stiff you can get falling asleep like that." She slid over into the corner, giving him more room.

He extended his legs. The muscles relaxed a little but now he realized how hungry he was.

"I'm surprised I fell asleep," he told her.

"It took me a few days before I could. I kept wondering if he'd come down to get me while I was sleeping. Finally I just couldn't stay awake anymore. Even being afraid didn't keep me awake. I guess you're braver than me."

"No," he said, "just older."

Gil wished he had been able to convince Kelly to untie him the night before. He would love to have stretched his arms.

"Kelly," he said, "have you thought about what we discussed? About untying me?"

"Yeah, I thought about it," she said, without looking at him.

"And?"

She continued to stare down at the floor, then lifted her head and looked at him with haunted eyes. "I'm just too scared. Sorry."

"Don't apologize," he said. "You have every right to be afraid, but do you just want to keep sitting here, waiting to see what's going to happen next?"

She didn't answer.

"Do you think you'll really be able to convince Jean that you love him, enough so he'll let you out of this cage?"

"It's my only chance. If I can get him to trust me, then he'll let me out, then I can run."

"Kelly," Gil said, "he's never going to trust you that much. You can't just keep hoping for something that's never going to happen. But together we can make something happen."

She drew her knees up to her chest and wrapped her arms around them.

He decided to try another tack.

"What if he does believe you and he lets you out? What if you get away? He's still going to hunt you down and try to kill you."

"I'll get help," she said, "and I'll send them back for you. Don't worry."

"It'll be too late. Once you're gone, he'll kill me right away—if he doesn't do it sooner. Maybe he'll decide to kill me and make you watch."

She hugged her knees tighter.

"I'm only here because I was looking for you," he said. "You wouldn't let me die, would you, Kelly?"

She started to cry. "I don't know what to do," she whispered. "I'm s-so scared."

"And you've been scared for a long time," he said. "But, honey . . . I think it's time to get mad, don't you?"

"Mad?"

"What right has he got to keep you here?" Gil asked. "What right did Auntie Laveau have to lock you up? What right does Jean have to keep you locked up after he got you away from her?"

She hesitated a moment, then said, "H-he's got no right."

"That's exactly it," Gil said. "No right at all. Look, if you untie me we'll have our best chance to get out of here. We've got to do it while I have some strength left. Jean's not that much bigger than me; I think we can both take him, if we have to. And once you untie me, we'll have the element of surprise on our side. I don't think he'd ever expect you to have the courage to plot against him."

He waited for some reaction, then decided to challenge her once more.

"He expects you to just sit here and wait for him, let him do whatever he wants to you. He thinks you have no guts at all, Kelly, but I know different."

She looked at him. "Y-you do?"

"I can see it in your eyes," Gil said. "He can't treat you this way and get away with it. Can he?"

She closed her hands into fists and brought them down on her knees. "He's got no right!" she hissed.

Gil thought he might have finally gotten through to her, but at exactly that moment the basement door opened and he lost any headway he might have made. The fear came rushing back and she sprang forward, grabbing the hood off the floor and jerking it back down over Gil's head.

CHAPTER 51

LASALLE HAD A BUSY MORNING. While Claire and Paul were wandering the Quarter, he went back to Rene Conde's building to talk with Raymelle Robicheaux and some of the other neighbors. But, as Raymelle had warned, no one else had anything to tell him.

"They all keep their shutters closed," she explained. "Me, I like the light, and I like to keep an eye on things."

She didn't have anything else to say on the subject. But LaSalle could overlook her reticence, since she had apparently gotten the plate numbers correctly off the gray car she'd spotted in the neighborhood earlier. When he ran them through the computer, it came up with the name William Jackson, living at an address in St. Claude.

Before checking it out, however, LaSalle had wanted to take a quick look inside Rene's apartment. He'd get nothing from the dead woman anymore, but perhaps there'd be something of interest in her home.

It was a small place and didn't take much time to check out. Once again, he did it without "tossing" it, although he did check inside cookie jars, canisters and books. He found nothing. Not an appointment book, phone book—nothing. Either Rene lived very sparsely, owning very little in the way of furniture and luxuries, or she had her good stuff stashed someplace else. Just factoring in what she had tried to pull on Gil and Claire Hunt, it wasn't hard to tell what she did for a living. She was a scam artist, and as such would have a safe place for her valuables.

They sure as hell weren't in her apartment on St. Anne.

All he had to go on was the fact that a black man had been in the neighborhood asking about Rene, and he'd been driving an eight-year-old gray Chevy Impala. Once LaSalle had William Jackson's name he was able to bring up the driver's license. He was a black male, so he could have been the man asking about Rene. On the other hand, somebody could have just been driving his car.

It was time to stop guessing, time to go see William Jackson and question him.

Claire and Paul ended up in Jackson Square, sitting on a step in front of the Cathedral. To try to keep his mother's mind occupied, Paul read out loud to her from one of the books he'd bought.

It described where and when Marie Laveau had been born, how many times she'd been married, how many children she had. It also told them about Marie's daughter, also named Marie, who had become almost as famous a voodoo witch as her mother.

Claire listened, not really paying attention. She loved Paul for trying, but the more he read, the more annoyed she became listening to him prattle on about Marie Laveau. How she had grown to hate that name.

Finally, she wasn't able to take it any longer. "Paul, it's all very interesting, but—"

He wasn't listening, however, and was now going on about other voodoo queens who had come after Marie Laveau. Suddenly what he said caught Claire's attention. "Wait a minute. What did you just say?"

"About what?"

"About other voodoo queens," Claire asked anxiously. "Read that part again."

"Uh . . ." Paul found the passage, and started reading aloud again until Claire interrupted him.

"That's the one. That name, Malvina Latour."

"What about it?"

"I've heard it before," she said, "at least the Latour part . . . wait, I know." She looked at Paul excitedly. "Detective LaSalle asked me if Gil had mentioned a name."

"Malvina Latour?"

"No, she said, "it was Latour but . . . not a woman . . . Jean! It was Jean Latour."

Quickly, Paul scanned ahead in the book. "I don't see anything about a Jean Latour, Mom."

"Well, Auntie Laveau's real name wasn't Laveau, so maybe this Jean Latour has another name, too. But the fact is LaSalle is looking for him."

"And he thought Gil might have known this guy?"

"Apparently," Claire said.

Paul wasn't sure where this was going, but it had brought the color back into his mother's face, and for that he was grateful.

"So," he said, standing up, "let's go."

"Go where?" she asked, as he helped her to her feet. "To find Jean Latour . . . who's connected to all these voodoo queens . . ."

Claire looked at Paul just as he looked at her. "Royalty!" she said.

"Kings and Queens, just like Von said. I bet if we find Jean Latour, he'll lead us to Gil," Paul said.

"But . . . where do we look?"

He smiled. "Where else? The phone book!"

CHAPTER 52

WILLIAM JACKSON LIVED in a run-down section of St. Claude, not far from the Desire Projects. LaSalle had been working solo for the past month because his partner had retired and a new one had not yet been assigned to him. But to drive over to St. Claude he had drafted a young detective named George de Buys. LaSalle didn't mind wandering the Quarter alone, but some of New Orleans's less desirable neighborhoods were better worked with a partner.

They approached the Jackson house and noticed a driveway leading to the back.

"Let's check this out," LaSalle said.

"Shouldn't we knock first and announce our arrival?" de Buys asked.

"Plenty of time to go by the book, George," LaSalle said. "Right now I want to make sure we've got the right place."

They walked down the dirt driveway and found an open garage with two cars inside and three outside. The car LaSalle was looking for was one of those outside.

"This must be the place," LaSalle said. "I ran Jackson's sheet and he's got a couple of priors for dealing in hot cars."

Even though the plate in question had not come back stolen, and did match the car it was attached to, LaSalle said, "I wonder what we'd find if we ran all these plates and vehicles?"

"Want me to go back to the car and radio them in?" de Buys asked, eagerly.

"No," LaSalle said. "If they come back hot, I don't want to be bogged down doing a ton of paperwork on stolen cars when I'm working a homicide."

De Buys looked disappointed, but did not argue. LaSalle looked inside the car, wishing he could get a quick peek inside the trunk.

"Hey!" a man's voice called out. They saw a gangly black man come running out the back door of the house. He was wearing a soiled white T-shirt and torn jeans. "Whatchoo wan' here, man?"

"We're looking for a car," LaSalle called back.

When the man reached them, LaSalle could see he was in his mid-twenties. Driver's-license photos being so bad, he couldn't tell if this was the man they were looking for, but the height, weight and age seemed correct. The stains on his shirt were fresh, some kind of grease glistened on his face and fingers. Apparently, noticing them in his backyard had interrupted his lunch.

"Lookin' ta buy a car, huh?" the man asked. "Somebody tell you 'bout me?"

"Yeah," LaSalle said, taking a shot, "I was told if I wanted to buy a used car that Willy Jackson could hook me up."

"You come to the right place, bro," Jackson said. "I can hook you up with anythin' you want."

"How about this one?" LaSalle asked, indicating the Impala.

"Naw, man, that one ain't for sale," Jackson said. "That one's mine."

"Is that a fact?" LaSalle asked. "Not for sale?"

"Ah said no." Jackson turned belligerent. "Hey, wait a minute. You dudes cops?"

"Good call, Willy," LaSalle said. He took out his badge and showed it to him; de Buys did the same.

"Hey, none of these cars be hot, man," Jackson said. "I gots them all fair an' legal."

"We're not here about hot cars, Willy," LaSalle said.

"Then what you here about?"

"This car was seen at the scene of a crime."

Jackson narrowed his eyes, on the alert for a con job, and asked, "What crime?"

"A woman got killed."

"Whoa, step back, bro," Jackson said. "I ain't done no murder, I ain't seen no murder—"

"I didn't say she was murdered," LaSalle said, cutting him off. "I said she was killed. Could have been an accident."

"Hit an' run?" Jackson asked, his eyes popping. He ran to the front of the car and pointed to the grille. "I ain't got no damage. See? Grille's okay, headlights—"

"Relax, Willy," LaSalle said, "I've got the feeling that maybe you loaned this car out to somebody yesterday. That's all I want to know about."

"Loaned it out?" Jackson asked, his eyes turning shifty. "Who'd I loan my ride out to, man? I don't loan my car out—"

"Not even to Jean Latour?" LaSalle asked.

Jackson hesitated only a second, and then said with disgust, "Ah, shit, man, what that bastard gone an' done in my car?"

"I don't know, Willy," LaSalle said, "but I want to find out. Why don't you pop the trunk for me . . . bro?"

CHAPTER 53

"DAMMIT," Claire said. She closed the phone book and looked at Paul, who was sitting on the other bed in her room.

"No Latours?" he asked.

"Too damn many. I thought it would be an unusual name, but this town is crawling with them."

"Let me have a look," he said, taking the book from her.

"Don't you trust me to look up a name?" she asked. "I'm not that far gone yet. Look for yourself; there's about a dozen."

"Yeah," Paul said, "but didn't you say that Auntie Laveau was killed in Algiers?"

"That's right."

"Well, let's see how many Latours there are in Algiers."

"Do you think it'll be in this book?" she asked.

"It's part of New Orleans, isn't it?"

"I suppose . . ."

She waited while Paul found the proper page and then moved his finger down the list.

"I don't see Algiers here, but there are three addresses that don't say exactly what part of the area they are."

He put the large book down on the table between the two beds and picked up the phone.

"What are you doing, Paul?" she asked, surprised.

"I'm going to call these three numbers and find out where they are."

"But . . . what are you going to say?"

"I don't know, but working all those hours telemarketing when I was in college is gonna come in handy now, I guess. Did I ever tell you I was voted most congenial?"

Claire watched her son, a look of wonder on her face. She knew, intellectually, that Paul was a grown man, but there were few times she actually saw him as such. Now as she watched him take charge, much as Gil would have done, the reality of the intelligent adult he was overwhelmed her.

"Well, that was a bust," he said, hanging up on the last call. "None of those were in Algiers."

"What if they were lying to you?" Claire asked.

"I don't see why they would. I was as charming as ever."

"Well, like you keep saying," Claire replied, "it was something to do. I just hope Detective LaSalle has better luck than we do and actually finds this Latour guy."

"I have an idea," Paul said, brightening up.

"Let's hear it. It has to be better than mine was."

"Let's go back to St. Anne Street," he said.

"What for? The woman is dead."

"Right, and we never got a chance to look around, or talk to anyone."

"But who would we talk to?"

"Neighbors, friends of the dead woman," he said. "Anyone we can find. Come on, Mom. Let's not give up."

"I'm not going to give up, honey," she said. "Not ever, until we find Gil."

"Besides," Paul said, "there's no such thing as a perfect crime. At least that's what one of my professors kept telling us. There's always a witness . . . somewhere. Or some little thing the killer left behind or forgot to cover up. We just have to find it."

St. Anne Street was turning out to be a bust, too. When they arrived, there was still yellow crime-scene tape tacked up on everything—the patio and the stairs leading up to Rene Conde's apartment.

"Should we go in anyway?" Paul asked.

"This isn't television, Paul," she said. "We could get arrested for interfering; besides . . . I don't know how to break and enter, do you?"

"Well . . . no. Okay, then we'll talk to the neighbors. Canvass the area."

"And say what?"

"Ask questions," Paul said. "Did anyone see Gil? We'll describe him."

"We're just going to knock on doors?"

"Sure, why not?" he asked. "It's just like making cold calls. Be pleasant—non-threatening. You know, just be yourself."

She thought a moment. "Well, all right," she said. "What have we got to lose?"

Knocking on doors seemed to be a bust as well. The people they spoke to swore they hadn't seen or heard anything.

And if they had, Claire and Paul soon figured out that not one of them would admit to it.

"This is the last one," Paul said. "We've talked to everyone who lives where they could have seen something."

"I hate to admit it, but I'm getting discouraged," Claire said.

"Come on, one more," Paul said and knocked.

An elderly black woman answered the door. "Yep, can I he'p you?"

"Ma'am," Claire began, for it was her turn to take the lead, "we'd like to ask you some questions about what happened to Rene Conde, in the courtyard next door to you?"

"Are you the police?" the woman asked. "I done talked to the police."

"No, we're not the police," Claire said. "We're looking for my husband. He's missing."

"Well, ain't that a shame," the woman said.

Claire knew that if she could play to the stranger's sympathy, she'd get some information. "Yes, it's been terrible. We have reason to believe he might have come to see Rene a few days ago."

"You don't want to talk about the day she died?"

"No, ma'am."

"Well, that's good," she said. "Nobody done ask me about any other day except the day she died. Ya'll come on in and I'll make some tea."

As they entered, she closed the door and said, "My name's Raymelle Robicheaux . . ."

CHAPTER 54

CLAIRE AND PAUL were very excited. Raymelle Robicheaux had described Gil perfectly, saying he had been at Rene's place two days before she died.

"Did you see where he went?" Claire asked. "Was he alone?"

"Ah'm sorry, dearie," Raymelle said, "but my phone rang and ah never did see him leave."

Claire and Paul thanked Raymelle for the information. As they were leaving, Raymelle grabbed Claire's arm and said, "Ah don' usually like white men, but that man of yours appeared ta be, seemed kinda—different."

Claire smiled and said, "Women do seem to like him."

On the street, Claire stopped. "Oh, I should have asked if we could use her phone."

"To call LaSalle?" Paul asked.

"Yes."

"Let's find a pay phone."

They found a bank of public phones in an alcove near an

ATM machine. Claire fished LaSalle's card out of her purse and dialed the number. A man answered, reporting that LaSalle was "out in the field."

"Would you please tell him Claire Hunt called and that I have some information about my husband? Thank you." She hung up and turned to Paul. "Now what do we do?"

"Well, we know that Rene was probably the last person to see Gil."

"And she's dead."

"I got an idea while you were on the phone."

"Let's hear it," she said. "I'll try anything."

"Let's go back to that shop, Accents, and talk to the owner."

"Nadine?" Claire didn't want to talk to her again. The woman had liked Gil too much, and in spite of everything that was happening, Claire felt jealous. "What for?"

"She said a few people worked for Auntie Laveau—made deliveries," Paul reminded her. "Maybe she knows Jean Latour."

That got Claire going again. "You're right," she said, grabbing his arm, "and maybe she knows where he lives."

"What are we waiting for?"

LaSalle stared into the trunk of the Impala and then looked at Willy Jackson.

"What?" Jackson asked. "What'd ya find?"

"Nothing," LaSalle said. "That's the problem."

"The lab could find something," Detective de Buys offered.

"Yeah, I'm sure they could, but that trunk is as beat up as the car. There's no carpet to grab fibers, it's greasy—if Gil

Hunt was in there, it left traces on him, not the other way around."

Before closing the trunk, LaSalle bent and inspected it again. This time he reached in, closed his eyes and ran his hand around the inside. It one of the corners he found something. A piece of cloth had snagged on a sharp edge. He pulled it off and stood up, holding it in the light. It was large enough to be a good-sized swatch, and it was the same color as the windbreaker he'd last seen Gil Hunt wearing.

"What's that?" Jackson asked.

"Looks like a piece of a man's jacket," LaSalle said. He looked at de Buys. "Could belong to Jean Latour, or to Gil Hunt."

"Or to Jackson, here," the younger detective said.

LaSalle looked at Jackson.

"Ain't mine," the black man said. "I ain't never been in that trunk."

"Willy," LaSalle said, "I need to find Jean Latour, and I need to find him in a hurry." Gil had already been missing too long to suit the detective. It seemed logical that the only reason someone would have taken him was to kill him. He might be dead already. But ever since finding the gray car described by Raymelle Robicheaux, LaSalle had been feeling a sense of urgency. Now, with the piece of torn jacket in his hand, it heightened.

"I—I can't . . ." Jackson said.

"You can do it here, or from a jail cell."

"Look," Jackson said, "his mama's some kinda voodoo queen, or somethin'. If I tell you where he lives, she'll hex me for sure."

"Not if I lock her up for kidnapping and murder," LaSalle said.

"You could do that?"

"To both of them," LaSalle said. "But I have to find them first."

Of course, all he'd be able to do when he found the pair was question them, but Jackson didn't have to know that.

"Well . . . I don't know exactly where he lives," Jackson said, "but he tol' me once that he lived across the alley from where he worked."

"And where did he work then?" LaSalle asked.

"For that other voodoo lady, the one calls herself Auntie Laveau."

Across the alley from the murder scene, LaSalle thought. He tried to conjure up a mental picture of the layout of the neighborhood, but he couldn't. Hell, Detective Mirel and his men had canvassed the area. Why hadn't anyone else pointed that out? Or was the whole neighborhood afraid of voodoo?

"Let's go," he said to de Buys.

"What about him?"

"Forget him."

De Buys ran to keep up with LaSalle. "Where are we going?"

"Algiers."

Paul waited outside the store while Claire went in to ask Nadine a few questions about her business dealings with Auntie Laveau. He looked at her anxiously as she came outside, her face flushed.

"What'd she say?"

"She said a black man made deliveries a couple of times and told her his name was Jean."

"Latour!" Paul said. "It's got to be. Does she know where he lives?"

"Not exactly," Claire said, "but she did say that they talked one time and he mentioned that he lived right near where he worked."

"We've got to call Detective LaSalle," Paul said.

"He's out in the field, remember?"

"Well, we've got to do something."

"And we are," she said. "Let's get a cab."

"Where are we going?" Paul asked.

"Algiers."

CHAPTER 55

BECAUSE CLAIRE AND Paul were in the Quarter and had no problem getting a cab, they arrived at the Algiers ferry quickly. They were already on board and the ferry was ready to disembark when LaSalle and de Buys arrived. Flashing their badges, they got on at the last minute.

Claire and Paul were seated inside, away from any of the windows, as they were not interested in sightseeing. Because of this, Claire spotted LaSalle as soon as he and his young partner-for-the-day appeared.

"Paul!" she said, grabbing his arm.

Paul looked at his mother, then in the direction she was pointing.

"What do you know," he commented. "I guess we're all out in the same field today."

Claire was about to wave to get the man's attention when LaSalle's eyes suddenly fell on her. He tugged at de Buys's arm and walked over.

"What are you two doing here?" he demanded.

"Going to Algiers," Claire said.

"Why?"

"Because Gil's there," Paul blurted out. He was eager to show that they knew something the police did not. It was a trait he shared with Gil. Claire had entertained the thought of lying to LaSalle, because she thought he'd try to stop them, but the cat was out of the bag now.

"And what makes you think that?" LaSalle asked.

"If you'll sit down and stop barking," Claire said to him, "we'll tell you."

LaSalle frowned. The ferry had already left, so there was no way to make the two get off. He sat down. De Buys remained standing. He and Paul seemed to be sizing each other up, as the young detective was only a few years older.

LaSalle was next to Claire, with Paul on the other side of her. De Buys took a seat away from all of them. He was lost, having not been introduced and still not sure who these people were, or even what case LaSalle was working on. He was simply along for the ride now.

"We were just looking for something to do, but . . ."

Claire went on to tell LaSalle everything they had done and found out, withholding nothing. He listened silently, taking everything in and weighing it all against what he had learned.

"And that's why we're going to Algiers," Claire finished. "Now, Detective, why are you going?"

LaSalle took a moment to decide just how much to tell her, and made the decision to be as honest as she had apparently been with him.

"All right," he said, "we have reason to believe—oh, this is Detective de Buys—we have reason to believe that Gil may be in a house on Algiers."

"The Latour house?" Claire asked.

"Yes," LaSalle said.

"Do you know about Malvina Latour, the voodoo queen?" Paul asked.

"Voodoo? We know that Jean Latour borrowed a car, was seen on St. Anne Street and may be the one who abducted Gil."

"Do you have his address?"

"No," LaSalle said, "but we were told the same thing you were, by a different source, that he lived very near the Laveau house."

Claire was more encouraged now than she had been in days.

"Mom?" Paul said, before she could speak again.

"What?"

"The water."

"What about it?"

"The card reader—remember what he said? We're on the water, and it's all around us."

"My God," she said.

"What's this about water?" LaSalle asked.

"Nothing," she said, not wanting him to think she was nuts. "Just something someone told us, it has nothing to do with Gil."

She looked out the window. The ride seemed endless. "How long does this take?" she asked.

"A few more minutes," LaSalle assured her. "But when we get there, I want you two to stay at the ferry station."

"What?" she asked. "Oh, no, if Gil is there, I'm going with—"

"Mrs. Hunt, I need you to do something for me," LaSalle said.

"What?"

"I need you to call a Detective Mirel of the local police and tell him I need backup." He could have found the

Algiers channel on his radio, but this would be a way to get her to stay behind. "We're going to need their help to search."

"He's right, Mom," Paul said.

She almost snapped at her son for taking the detective's side, but realized they were both right.

"Besides," LaSalle added, "if we run into a dangerous situation I don't want to have to worry about you."

"All right, all right," she said grudgingly.

By the time the ferry docked, he had found the phone number and handed it to her.

"When you find Gil," she said to LaSalle, "don't let anything happen to him."

"I won't."

"Do you swear?" She knew her tone was strident, her request unreasonable, but she wanted to hear him say it.

"Mrs. Hunt," he said, "I swear."

CHAPTER 56

IT SURPRISED GIL when Kelly suddenly skittered over to his side of the cage. She'd been keeping her distance from him the whole time he'd been there.

"What are you doing?" he asked.

"I'm going to untie you."

Apparently she'd been thinking about his proposal and trying to get up the courage.

As if reading his mind, she added, "I have to do it quickly before I lose my nerve."

It was all he could do not to cry out, "It's about time!" He watched helplessly as she fumbled with the knots, her fingers cramped from constantly keeping them balled up in fists. He wanted to yell at her to hurry, but knew that would only rattle her. All at once a feeling of dread and urgency shrouded him. Without knowing why, he knew they needed to be ready to move very soon.

The four of them got off the ferry together. LaSalle turned

to Claire and handed her the swatch of cloth he'd taken from the trunk of Willy Jackson's car.

"That's what led me here," he said and told her where he'd found it.

She held the scrap in the palm of her hand. "It's from Gil's jacket. I always hated that jacket." She smiled sadly.

"I thought so."

She closed her hand into a fist and held it that way, eyes shut tightly.

"Make that call for me, Mrs. Hunt," LaSalle said. He turned and looked at de Buys. "Let's go. We can walk it from here." Then he looked at Paul. "Whatever you do, keep your mother here, where she'll be safe."

"I will," Paul said.

There was a pay phone near the dock area. Claire and Paul walked over and she made the call. It took a few minutes to get Detective Mirel on the phone and even more time to convince him that she was telling the truth.

"Why can't you just go over there and then decide if I'm lying later?" she demanded. "Detective LaSalle told me to ask for you specifically. How would I know your name if he hadn't told me?"

"All right, ma'am," he said finally. "I'll round up some men and get over there—but if this is a false report, you could be in a lot of trouble."

"Oh, just go!" she snapped, and hung up the phone with a bang. Folding her arms across her chest, she stared out across the water, studying the riverfront of New Orleans. "Now what? I can't just stand here and—wait a minute."

"What?"

She turned toward her son, a look of wonder on her face. "First the royalty, now the water."

Paul couldn't help but smile. "You're not telling me you believe—"

"Before we left the museum," she said, cutting him off, "the man told me to always choose the middle."

"Yeah, I know. What do you think that means?"

"I'm not sure, but suddenly I have such an anxious feeling in the pit of my stomach." Her heart was pounding wildly. Gil was near. She knew it! "It's like I can almost feel Gil. His fear. His sadness."

Paul felt so powerless watching his mother. "Sorry, Mom, but I don't—"

"What if LaSalle ends up in the right neighborhood but at the wrong house?" she asked. "What if he's too late to save Gil? But what if Gil *could* have been saved if only LaSalle had known enough to . . ."

Paul finished her thought, ". . . choose the middle . . ."

She grabbed his arm. "We have to catch up to them!"

CHAPTER 57

WHEN SHE FINALLY GOT HIM free, Gil panicked because he couldn't feel his arms, let alone move them. He didn't want her to see, so he started slowly, first with his fingers.

"What's wrong?" she asked.

"I've been tied up for days. It'll take a while . . . don't worry."

"Here," she said, frantically grabbing one of his arms, "I can rub them—that'll get the blood moving."

When she raised his arm, he wanted to cry out in pain, but he didn't dare. He feared that Jean might come running down the stairs and drag him from the cage before he was able to defend himself.

As Kelly rubbed one arm and then the other, a thousand needles pricked his skin as the feeling began to return. He was able once again to move his fingers and started clenching and unclenching his fists.

"How are you?" she asked, concerned.

"Better," he said through clenched teeth, "thank you."

He'd lost track of time, didn't know if they were near a

mealtime or not. If Jean came down now to bring Kelly some food . . .

"All right," Gil said, reclaiming his arms and shaking them out. "Let's take a look at this."

He moved to the door of the cage and was shocked at what he found. "What the hell—" he said, looking at Kelly. "It's not locked."

"I know."

He turned to face her. "You could have left anytime?"

"No," she said. "There used to be a padlock on there, but he took it off for some reason."

"When?"

"Just a few days ago."

"So you still could have left."

"No . . . I—couldn't."

He stared at her. Was she so paralyzed by fear that she couldn't even go through an unlocked door? Then again, she'd still have to make her way up the stairs and out of the house. He hoped it was just fear that had kept her there, and not some variation of the Stockholm syndrome he'd been reading so much about.

Well, no matter what had kept her inside that cage, he knew the most difficult task he faced right now was getting her to walk past the bars.

"Come on, Kelly," he said gently, "you can do it."

Upstairs, Malvina Latour looked over at her son, who was sitting at the kitchen table drinking coffee.

"What's it gon' be, boy?" she asked.

"Mama?"

"Whatchoo gon' do wit' dat girl?"

"Gonna keep her, Mama," he said. "I told you before, I love her."

"She love you, you t'ink?"

"She will."

Mama Latour shook her head. What made men so stupid when it came to women? she wondered.

"Well, den, you got to get rid of dat man," she said. "I don' be keepin' dem both here."

"I get rid of him, Mama."

"Today," she said.

"Today," he repeated, bobbing his head.

She walked over to her boy, put her hands on his shoulders and said, "You finish dat coffee, you, and den you get rid of him."

"Where?"

"I don't care where," she said. "Jus' you stay away from dat Laveau house. Dem police already find dem girls."

"All right, Mama."

"A good boy, you," she said, patting his back.

"You know where this house is?" Detective de Buys asked, trying to keep up with LaSalle.

"I know where the Laveau house is located," LaSalle said. "After that we'll have to start scouting the area."

"Before backup gets here?" de Buys asked.

"You can't always wait for backup."

"The book says—"

"Can't always go by the book, either, George," LaSalle told the young detective. "A lot of people would be dead if I only went by the book."

"But I—"

"Just follow my lead, George," LaSalle said over his shoulder. "Just keep an eye on me and follow my lead."

"How do we know which way they went?" Paul asked.

They'd left the ferry landing behind them and were trying to catch up to LaSalle and de Buys.

"I thought they came this way," Claire said, looking around.

Paul stood with his hands on his hips. "Well, he did say it was in walking distance."

"Let's just keep moving in this direction, Paul. They can't be that far ahead of us."

Paul didn't want to say anything to discourage his mother. But at the rate LaSalle and de Buys were walking and the amount of time Claire had spent on the phone, he feared they might never find the two men. Even if he and his mother were walking in the wrong direction, however, at least they were together and he could keep her safe. LaSalle and de Buys were the pros, after all. They'd save Gil.

"I can't," Kelly said.

"Yes, you can," Gil encouraged. "All you have to do is crawl out the door and you're free."

"What if he comes down?"

"If he does, there's two of us and only one of him. We can handle him."

"But his mama—"

"Has she ever come down here?"

"No," Kelly admitted.

"All right, then. Look, I'll go first, and then you follow."

She nodded.

He turned, opened the door and crept out onto the basement floor. Once there, he turned and put his hand out to her. "Come on, Kelly," he said. "How long has it been since you went anywhere on your own? Of your own free will?"

She stared at him, at his hand, then closed her eyes and took a deep breath. With her lids pressed together, she reached out for his hand. He grabbed her and tugged gently, bringing her first up to the doorway and then through it.

"Open your eyes," he said.

She hesitated, then opened them and looked around.

"You're out. See?"

She looked amazed. "I'm out?"

"We both are," he said. "Now let's see if there's another way out of here."

CHAPTER 58

THE BASEMENT RAN **the length of the small house, but there were no doors other than the one at the top of the stairs. The windows were all too small for either of them to fit through.**

"Only one way in or out," Gil said.

"What do we do now?"

"Shhh. Wait a minute." He held up his hand. "I think I heard something."

They stood frozen, listening intently for any sign of habitation upstairs. Finally they heard footsteps, and then the scraping of a chair across the floor.

"They're home!" Kelly said.

Gils' stomach churned. He'd been hoping that no one would be in the house and they'd be able just to walk right out of there. But deep in his heart he knew that was way too much to hope for.

"What do we do now?" she asked urgently.

"We'll have to surprise him when he comes down," Gil said.

"How?"

"Well, first," Gil said, "I guess we have to get back inside that damn cage."

Kelly turned and looked at the bars with wide, fearful eyes. But within a matter of seconds, her expression became enraged. "No!"

"Kelly—"

She turned her anger on him. "You wanted me to get mad. Well, I'm mad, and I am not getting back into that thing now that I'm out."

"But, Kelly, we—"

"I'd rather die."

He looked at her and saw the resolve not only in her face, but surging through her body. "All right, give me a minute to think of something else."

"This is the block," LaSalle said, stopping only to make sure de Buys was next to him. "The house is this way." He pointed straight ahead.

"Are we after one man?" de Buys asked.

"I think so," LaSalle said, "and possibly a woman."

De Buys took out his gun.

"I want them alive, if possible," LaSalle said. "I've got a lot of questions that need answering."

He could see in de Buys's eyes that the younger man was still worried about backup.

"Look," he said, "you can stay here and try to get the Algiers station on your radio. I'll go on alone."

"No," de Buys said, "you had Mrs. Hunt call. Besides, we don't know how close we are and these radios have pretty loud static. Someone might hear us coming."

"All right, then," LaSalle said, "but holster your gun. I don't want any accidents."

De Buys hesitated, then put his gun away.

"Which way?" Paul asked aloud, and she could hear the rising panic in his voice.

They had come to a fork.

"We could split up," Claire suggested.

"No!"

"It's the only way, Paul."

"I am *not* leaving you, Mom," he said. "I love Gil and I want to help him, but . . . you're my ..." He couldn't finish his sentence.

She hesitated and kept herself from reaching out to touch his face. This was no time for a tender moment.

"Okay," she said, "then run ahead down that street and look around the corner, see if you can spot them."

He did as she said, racing down the street that curved left. It wasn't long before he came running back.

"It doesn't look residential." He bent over, trying to catch his breath.

"Then our decision is made for us," she said. "We go right."

Jean stood up from the table.

"You go down now?" his mother asked.

"Wait," he said.

He walked to the closet on the other side of the room, took out something wrapped in a towel. Tossing the towel back into the closet, he gripped a wicked-looking machete in his right hand.

"Is dat what you used on dem girls?" she asked.

"Yes."

She walked up to him and smacked his face.

"What was that for?" he cried.

"You keep a murder weapon in me closet, you? Why you do such a t'ing?"

"Mama—"

"You use it on dat man, den you get rid of him and it, you understand what I'm sayin' to you?"

"Yes, Mama."

"Now you go."

Jean tightened his grip on the machete and walked to the basement door.

CHAPTER 59

GIL AND KELLY couldn't tell what was being said. Then they heard footsteps, and the basement door opened.

"He's coming!" she hissed.

"Kelly," Gil whispered, "let's jump him, put him in the cage and see how he likes it, okay?"

She blinked several times, fighting back the fear and panic that grew inside her like a thundering tornado. "Okay."

"You're not alone in this, remember? We're in this together," he said, trying to encourage her.

Carefully he went and stood to the right of the stairs. Then, pointing to the other side, said, "You stand over there. When Jean comes down, we'll grab him." Gil didn't know how much strength he and Kelly would be able to muster in a struggle, he just hoped that between them it would be enough. Because they would probably only get one chance at this.

"There it is," LaSalle said, seeing the Laveau house ahead.

There was a slight breeze and what was left of the yellow crime-scene tape rippled.

They walked up to the front of the house. There were no houses to either side of it. Checking around the back, they noticed that there wasn't even a real alley, just a wide dirt path running along the back of the property. But set back, on the other side of the path, were five houses.

"Which one?" de Buys asked.

"We'll have to go door to door," LaSalle said. "We'll split up."

"Split up?"

LaSalle turned to look at de Buys, and that was when he caught sight of Claire and Paul almost running up the street.

"What the—"

"There they are," Paul said. "They're going into the back-yard of that house."

"Thank God we found them." Claire was still clutching the torn piece from Gil's jacket in her hand.

LaSalle faced them, anger making a muscle in his jaw jump.

"I thought I told you—"

"The middle one," Claire said.

"What?"

She turned and looked across the path at the five houses.

"Go to the middle one first," she said, pointing. "Please."

"That's what you came running to tell us?"

"Yes," Paul said, less out of breath than his mother. "We believe the middle one is the Latour house."

"How—"

"What does that matter? We're wasting time," Paul said urgently.

"It couldn't hurt to start with the middle one," de Buys said.

LaSalle took a deep breath, then slowly let it out. "All right. All right."

They started toward the path. LaSalle stopped short and said to Claire, "Oh, no, you're not coming."

"Try and stop me," she said.

He looked at Paul, but the resolve in his eyes matched his mother's.

"Let's go," LaSalle said disgustedly.

CHAPTER 60

JEAN TURNED ON the basement light and started down the steps. What Gil could not have known was that from that angle, Jean could see right into the cage. He stopped halfway down when he saw it was empty.

"Where are you?"

Gil watched Kelly, bringing his finger to his lips. Maybe Jean would come down the rest of the way to investigate.

"Kelly?"

Gil saw the frightened girl stiffen at the sound of her name.

"Kelly," Jean called again. "Come out where I can see you."

Gil watched, hoping the girl would be able to resist.

"You can't get away from me, Kelly," Jean said. "My mama said a spell so you'll always want to be with me."

Gil tried catching her eye to give her some sort of encouragement, but she wasn't looking at him. She didn't seem to be looking at anything in particular but stood dazed.

"Kelly," Jean said, "you have to come out."

Gil watched helplessly as Kelly gave in to her fear and stepped out into the open.

"I don't blame you, sweetheart," Jean said, "it isn't your fault. Where is the man?"

Gil's feelings of helplessness increased as Kelly turned, looked at him and pointed.

Claire, Paul, LaSalle and de Buys approached the middle house, a small A-frame similar to all the others in the area, including the Laveau house.

"Stay here," LaSalle said to de Buys.

"Right."

De Buys put his hand on the holster under his jacket, but didn't draw his gun.

LaSalle, Claire and Paul mounted the porch. The detective knocked.

"Kelly," Jean said, "get back in the cage."

Gil tried not to get angry at the girl. She'd been Jean's prisoner for a long time, he reasoned, and probably thought she had no choice but to obey him. He watched as she fell down on her knees and crawled back behind the bars. Remembering how she'd refused to get back in for him, claiming that she'd rather die, he knew her fear must have been beyond his comprehension.

Now he was alone, left to deal not only with Jean, but with his own fear as well.

The door was opened by a very large, fat black woman wearing what Claire could only call a muumuu. There probably wasn't much else that would fit her. Her upper arms were huge, the skin dimpled with cellulite. Her black hair was shot with gray. Her eyes, however, were striking. They were piercing, steady, and projected great confidence.

"Can I help you?" she asked.

LaSalle had instructed Claire to initiate the conversation, hoping the party inside would feel less threatened by a woman. "Are you Mrs. Latour?" she asked.

"Some call me Mama Latour. Me name is Malvina."

Claire hoped she hid her shock. Malvina Latour was the same name as the voodoo queen she'd read about who had succeeded Marie Laveau. Her heart was beating wildly. She was sure now that Gil was in this house somewhere.

"How can I help you?" Mama Latour asked.

"Well, actually," Claire said, "I was looking for your son."

"He is not here."

"Do you know where he is?" LaSalle asked.

Mama Latour studied the man a minute before saying, "I don't know. Dat boy, he got a mind all his own, him do."

LaSalle had no warrant to enter the house, and if she didn't want to give up her son, he couldn't make her—unless he had probable cause.

"Give me your name, I make sure he call you," the older woman said. "But I can't be standin' in me door all day." Claire looked at LaSalle. What was he waiting for?

"Come on, now, mister."

Gil decided he was going to have to try to go hand-to-hand with Jean without Kelly's help. He hadn't eaten in days, he was weak, and he had never been, nor ever had reason to be, much of a fighter. He only hoped that battling for his life would trigger off something, that the terror would somehow give him an edge.

"Okay, you take your time, mister," Jean said. "I can wait. I can sit up here all day 'cause I ain't cornin' down there. You think I'm stupid, mister? Like all them others? You think I don't know if I come down there you gonna jump me?"

"A-all right," Gil said, annoyed that his voice cracked. "I'll come out."

He stepped into Jean's field of vision and his blood went cold when he saw the man was holding a machete.

CHAPTER 61

AFTER MAMA LATOUR closed the front door, she hurried to the kitchen as fast as she could. Who did they think they were kidding? She knew that the tall man was a policeman. She had to warn her baby boy.

"We'll call back again?" Claire asked LaSalle as they walked away from the house. "Why did you tell her that?"

"Why didn't we just go in?" Paul asked impetuously.

"We have no warrant," Detective de Buys explained, "and no probable cause. We can't just break into someone's house."

"My partner is quoting the book," LaSalle said.

"To hell with your book," Claire said. "My husband is in that house. He may be in danger this very minute."

"What makes you so sure of that?" de Buys asked. "Are you psychic?"

"Detective LaSalle," she said, ignoring de Buys's sarcasm, "didn't I tell you the middle house belonged to the Latours?"

"Yes, you did . . ."

"Well, we can't just walk away without doing something," she complained.

"We're not, Mrs. Hunt."

"What?"

"Now that we know this is the Latour house," LaSalle explained, "we're going to have a look around . . . outside."

"You mean you're not just walking away?"

"No, I'm not. You see, I also think your husband is in there, but I have no evidence. Once I do, we can go in."

"LaSalle—" de Buys started.

"Don't quote the book to me again, George," LaSalle said. "If you want, stay out in front."

"You can't—" de Buys started, but LaSalle was already moving around to the side of the house, with Claire and Paul in pursuit. De Buys felt he had no choice but to follow.

Jean pointed at Gil with the machete.

"I shoulda kilt you right away."

Gil didn't answer. His mouth was too dry to form words. He could hear Kelly whimpering in the corner of the cage and knew she was going to be of no help to him.

Suddenly, the basement door flew open. A woman hissed down to Jean, "Dat was da police at da door. You gon' kill him, you got to do it quiet!"

Jean looked up at her. Gil saw this as his only chance. While Jean was answering his mother, Gil charged.

He had to run almost halfway up the steps, his shoes scraped the wood, giving Jean a warning. Fear made Gil move faster than he ever moved before. He locked his arms around Jean's legs before the man could react. Jean brought the machete down on Gil's back, but in his haste he did so hilt-first. Gil cried out as the handle dug into his skin. His feet slipped on the stairs and he started to fall backward. He held tightly to Jean's legs and took the man with him. Although his strength could not match the younger man's, his superior weight worked to his advantage and they both tumbled down the stairs.

Gil's elbow struck the basement floor hard, but he was too panicky to feel much. He had no way of knowing if the fall had separated Jean from his machete.

If Mama Latour had been right, then there were policemen in the area. He briefly thought that what he should have done was yell, but it had never occurred to him during the fall, and then he was occupied by the ensuing fight.

He rolled on the floor, then righted himself and got to his knees. He searched frantically for Jean and the machete and saw that they had, indeed, parted company.

Jean was on his knees as well. Their eyes locked for a moment, and then they both scrambled for the knife.

Mama Latour knew that she could not get down the stairs to help her son. She was too fat, probably would have fallen to her death. Instead, she turned, ran back through the kitchen and headed for her altar. She had in mind a quick hex that might help her boy, but she had to act fast.

Gil knew just a moment of triumph as his hand closed on the hilt of the machete, but the next second he felt Jean's arm come across his throat from behind, and then the man was sitting on him, choking the life out of him. Lying flat on the hard floor beneath the black man's weight, he could not bring the machete to bear. He'd saved himself from the blade, but spots began to appear before his eyes and he realized he was being strangled.

LaSalle bent to peer through one of the small louver-style basement windows, but they were so filthy he couldn't see a thing. Eventually, they reached the back of the house. It was only one story high, but had been raised up off the ground by its foundation, and even he was unable to stand high enough on his toes to see inside.

"Now what do we do?" Claire asked desperately. She suddenly felt as if she were gasping for air.

"We need probable cause," LaSalle said, looking at his by-the-book partner, who would give him up in a minute if he broke into this house illegally. "Probable cause."

"God," Claire said, feeling as if she was going to pass out, "something's wrong."

The last thing she heard was Paul shouting, "Mom!"

Gil tried desperately to get at Jean with the machete but the man had his head buried in the left side of Gil's neck as he continued to squeeze with his forearm. He was able to hit him a couple of blows on the back, but they had no effect on the pressure that was being applied to his neck.

He'd be dead in minutes if he didn't do something. His heart was beating so fast he thought he might pass out before he died. He opened his mouth to cry out, but nothing but a croak came out.

Then he saw Kelly.

She was in the cage, holding her knees to her chest, rocking, watching the struggle with wide eyes. It was as if his vision sharpened and he could see the cords standing out on her neck.

She was trying to scream.

"Scream . . . Kelly," he tried to tell her. It was his only chance. If she screamed, the police might hear. "Come . . . on . . . scream . . . damn . . . it . . ."

Suddenly, a deep black hole opened up and he fell into it. There was a pinprick of light at the end, but as he fell he didn't seem to be getting closer to it, and it didn't seem to be getting any brighter. He was calm now, almost happy. Floating . . . gliding . . .

The air was pierced by a high-pitched, bloodcurdling scream. He hoped it wasn't too late because the hole was closing in around him.

Outside, LaSalle, de Buys, Paul and Claire heard a scream.

"That's it!" LaSalle said; his prayers for probable cause had been answered. He took out the back door with one lunge.

CHAPTER 62

WHEN GIL OPENED HIS EYES, Claire was looking down at him, stroking his hair. Although her lips were smiling, he could tell she had been crying.

"There you are," she said. "You came back to me."

"I love you," he said.

She leaned over and kissed him. He could taste her tears.

Having said that to his wife and feeling that it was safe, he asked, "What the hell happened?"

She told him that, after LaSalle had smashed in the back door, he and his partner entered the house. They found Mama Latour at a voodoo altar, apparently casting some kind of a spell. LaSalle told de Buys to watch her and followed the direction of the screams, which still continued.

LaSalle found the basement door, rushed down and tried to pull Jean Latour off Gil. When the young man would not release his stranglehold, LaSalle had to take out his gun and strike the man several times on the head before he finally let go . . .

"He saved your life," Claire said. "Well, he and Kelly did. If she hadn't screamed—"

"She screamed?"

"Loud and clear."

"I can't believe it," he said, looking proud. "She did it."

"Yeah, but once she got started, the poor thing couldn't stop," Claire said sadly. "She screamed all the way here."

"Kelly's here?"

"Right down the hall. Relax," she said, pushing him back down into the pillows.

"How is she?" he asked, almost afraid to hear the answer.

"The bruises have pretty much healed. She was dehydrated and malnourished. The hospital has arranged for her to see a therapist. It'll take time, but I think she'll be fine. She's been asking to see you. I'll wheel you down there when you're stronger."

"Stronger?"

"You're in the hospital, hon," she said.

Gil looked at her puzzled, unable to put everything she was telling him in the right order.

Seeing his confusion, she started again, slower this time. "Paul's outside. He's been so worried about you. He loves you so much, you know?"

"Yeah, I know. He's a good kid," he said. "What about everyone . . . else?"

"Mama Latour and her son Jean were arrested. Detective LaSalle said he'd stop by as soon as you woke up."

"So . . . how long have I been here?"

"That's the scary part, Gil," she said. "You've been in a coma for a week—well, the doctors didn't call it that, but you've been unconscious."

"What exactly did the doctors say?"

"You know how vague they can be. I'd ask a question and they'd avoid answering it. They just seemed puzzled. I got the feeling they were trying to prepare me in case you never woke up. But I knew you'd come back to me." She took his hand and squeezed it tightly.

"You're stuck with me, Claire," he said. "Strange, though, I dreamed about you, I think. I mean, I thought I heard you . . . talking."

"I have been. I've been here every day—talking, reading. And when I wasn't, Paul was. We both knew if we kept up the noise, you'd work your way back to the top."

Gil's eyes felt heavy and he was barely able to say how tired he was before he fell asleep.

The next time Gil woke up he stayed awake for a while longer. It was later the same day, and this time LaSalle and Paul were there with Claire.

"How you doin', G-Man?" Paul asked.

"I'm fine, Stick Boy. How are you?"

"Better, now. Lots better."

LaSalle said, "It's good to see your eyes open, Mr. Hunt. You reminded me of Rene Conde for a while there."

"Jesus," Gil said, "was I . . ." He didn't dare say it. It sounded too . . . weird.

"Well, the old lady, Mama Latour," LaSalle said, "she claims she hexed you while you were fighting with her son. We caught her at her altar, but she said it was too late. She said you'd never wake up."

Gil shifted in bed, trying to get comfortable. "I'm glad she was wrong."

"Do you want to sit up?" Claire asked.

"That'd be nice."

She pushed a button on a control panel by the bed, moving it into an upright position, then fluffed his pillows for him.

"Thanks. Is there—was there anything else wrong with me?"

"Well, LaSalle said, "you were dirty and you stunk pretty bad—"

"You slept through all the sponge baths the pretty nurses gave you," Paul teased.

"I really must have been out of it." Gil winked at Paul.

"You were suffering from a mild case of malnutrition," LaSalle continued, "and your neck was badly bruised.

"Yeah," Gil said, touching it, "my throat is still pretty sore. I am hungry, though."

"Oh, he's feeling a lot better," Paul said.

"Well," LaSalle said, "I should leave you with your family."

Gil grabbed the man's sleeve. "Wait, I've got some questions."

"And I've got the answers . . . well, most of them." LaSalle pulled up a chair. "What do you want to know?"

Claire sat on one corner of Gil's bed while Paul sat on the other. "Yeah, I want to know why Marie Laveau was kidnapping those girls," Claire asked.

"Slave labor, power, lots of crazy reasons," LaSalle said. "It's something she was doing for quite some time, one girl at a time. But we do know that Kelly Denoux didn't have any family looking for her, so they thought they'd be safe."

"Kelly told me some of that," Gil said. "Jean fell in love

with her, fought with Auntie when she ordered him to kill Kelly. Then he took her with him to his mother's house, thinking he was giving her a better life . . . with him."

"Apparently his mother had him working for Auntie to spy on her," LaSalle said. "The neighbors, now that both women are gone, won't stop talking. They say the women were sort of rivals—dueling voodoo queens."

"What about Rene Conde?" Claire asked. "Was she into all that voodoo stuff, too?"

"No, but she was the only one they feared might give them up," LaSalle said. "They wanted to kill her, but she just happened to die on her own."

"On her own?" Gil asked. "What do you mean?"

"Jean went to kill her but when he saw you with her, he grabbed you—drugged you with some ether derivative his mother kept around. He was supposed to go back and kill Rene, but she died."

"That poor woman," Gil said. "I had no idea."

"I knew it had to be natural causes," Claire said.

"Well." LaSalle looked at Paul and Claire, and then back to Gil. "The M.E. still doesn't see any reason why she should have died, and now that Mama Latour is in custody, she's claiming she hexed Rene."

"Anybody believe that one?" Gil asked.

LaSalle said, "There's got to be some logical explanation."

They all fell silent for a few seconds.

"So," Gil said, "who found me?"

"Oh, we all did that," Paul said. "Wait until we tell you about the tarot reading Mom had."

"Your wife and stepson did some outstanding amateur police work and got to the Algiers ferry the same time I did. For some reason, your wife seemed to know the exact house you were being held in. If we'd had to go house to house, you'd have been dead by the time we found you."

Gil looked at Claire, who said, "I found out about Algiers from your new friend Nadine."

"Who?" Gil asked.

"We'll talk later."

LaSalle stood. "Well, I'd better get going. Any more questions, Gil, and we can talk when you get out."

Gil extended his hand. "Thank you."

"Don't thank me," LaSalle said. Your wife had more to do with it than anyone. She can be quite a bully when she doesn't get her way."

"I'm going to take that as meaning that I'm a determined, strong-willed woman," Claire said.

"I meant it that way." LaSalle released Gil's hand and got a quick hug from Claire.

"You're a lucky man, Gil," he said. "You've got quite a family here."

"Don't I know it."

LaSalle waved good-bye to Paul and went out the door.

"Come here, you," Gil said, opening his arms to Claire.

"Looks like my cue to check out the cafeteria," Paul said and hurried out of the room.

She buried her face in his neck. Beneath the antiseptic smell she found the sweet muskiness of his skin. "The oddest thing happened outside that house," she said. "I could feel you. I was choking and I knew you were, too."

He leaned back to look into her eyes. "Well, we both know we have this . . . connection."

"But I fainted, Gil. I still feel guilty fainting when you needed me. But as near as we can reconstruct it, I passed out the same time you blacked out."

"Honey"—he hugged her—"you did fine; stop worrying about it."

She pushed away from him. "Don't you see? If we believe that somehow we're psychically linked, how far are we from believing in voodoo and hexes?"

"And ghosts?" he laughed.

"I'm serious, Gil."

"Claire, look at me. I'm awake. If any voodoo queen hexed me, it didn't hold."

"Well, I'll tell you one thing," she said. "It's going to be a long time before I let you talk me into getting involved in any kind of a mystery again."

"You'll get no argument there," he said.

BIBLIOGRAPHY

Asbury, Herbert. *The French Quarter*. Alfred A. Knopf, Inc., 1936.

Courtaway, Robbi. *Spirits of St. Louis*. Virginia Publishing Corp., 1999.

Flake, Carol. *New Orleans*. Grove Press, 1994.

Guiley, Rosemary Ellen. *Harper's Encyclopedia of Mystical Paranormal Experience*. HarperCollins Publishers, 1991.

Longo, Jim. *Ghosts Along the Mississippi* (Haunted Odyssey II) Ste. Anne's Press, 1993.

Martinez, Raymond J. *Mysterious Marie Laveau Voodoo Queen*. Hope Publications.

Pelton, Robert W. Voodoo Signs and Omens. A. S. Barnes and Co., Inc., 1974.

Tallant, Robert. *The Voodoo Queen*. Putnam, 1956.

A LOOK AT: SAME TIME, SAME MURDER (GIL & CLAIRE 3)

When Gil and Claire Hunt signed up to attend a mystery writers' convention, the last thing they expected to encounter was a real-life murder. But when the convention's star attraction, prominent hardboiled writer Robin Everly, is found dead in his hotel room, Gil and Claire find themselves hunting for a clever killer.

AVAILABLE NOVEMBER 2018

ABOUT THE AUTHORS

Randisi was born and raised in Brooklyn, N.Y., and from 1973 through 1981 he was a civilian employee of the New York City Police Department, working out of the 67th Precinct in Brooklyn. After 41 years in N.Y, he now resides in Laughlin, NV, 90 miles South of Las Vegas, on the Colorado River, with his 25-year partner-in-life-and-crime, Marthayn Pelegrimas.

He is the author of the "Miles Jacoby," "Nick Delvecchio," "Joe Keough," and "Dennis McQueen," mystery series, and the co-author of the "Gil & Claire Hunt" series. He has been nominated four times for the Shamus Award from the Private Eye Writers of America, in the Novel and Short Story categories.

For more information:
https://wolfpackpublishing.com/robert-j-randisi/

CHRISTINE MATTHEWS has published over sixty stories under her real name, Marthayn Pelegrimas, as well as her "Matthews" mystery pseudonym. She has appeared in *Alfred Hitchcock's Mystery Magazine, Deadly Allies II, Ellery Queen's Mystery Magazine, Lethal Ladies, For Crime Out Loud I & II, Mickey Spillane's Vengeance Is Hers, Cat Crimes On Holiday, Till Death Do Us Part, Hollywood and*

Crime and *Crime Square*. Her stories have been chosen five times for Ed Gorman and Martin H. Greenberg's Best of the Year books, the most recent being the 2011 edition. She is the author of four novels and the editor of several anthologies.

www.ingramcontent.com/pod-product-compliance
Lightning Source LLC
Chambersburg PA
CBHW021005260626
47169CB00006B/1946